By What Authority?
Part III

by
Robert Hugh Benson

By What Authority?
Part III
by Robert Hugh Benson

Copyright © 2024

All Rights reserved.

No part of this publication may be reproduced, stored in a retrieval system, or transmitted in any form or by any means, electronic, mechanical, photocopying or Otherwise, without the written permission of the publisher.
The author/editor asserts the moral right to be identified as the author/editor of this work.

ISBN: 978-93-67141-97-7

Published by
DOUBLE 9 BOOKS
2/13-B, Ansari Road
Daryaganj, New Delhi – 110002
info@double9books.com
www.double9books.com
Tel. 011-40042856

This book is under public domain

ABOUT THE AUTHOR

Robert Hugh Benson was an English Catholic priest and author who lived from 18 November 1871 to 19 October 1914. He began his ministry as an Anglican priest before being welcomed and ordained in the Catholic Church in 1903. He also wrote a lot of fiction, including Come Rack! Come to Rope! and the well-known dystopian novel Lord of the World. His works include current fiction, children's stories, plays, apologetics, devotional writings, and historical, horror, and science fiction. In parallel with rising through the ranks to serve as a Chamberlain to Pope Pius X in 1911 and earning the title of Monsignor before passing away a few years later, he continued his writing career. Benson, the younger brother of E. F., A. C., and Margaret Benson, was the youngest child of Edward White Benson, the Archbishop of Canterbury, and his wife, Mary. Robert Hugh Benson attended Eton College for his education before attending Trinity College in Cambridge from 1890 to 1893 to study classics and religion. Benson's father, who was the Archbishop of Canterbury at the time, gave him his ordination as a priest in the Church of England in 1895.

CONTENTS

CHAPTER I
THE COMING OF SPAIN 7

CHAPTER II
MEN OF WAR AND PEACE 13

CHAPTER III
HOME-COMING 25

CHAPTER IV
STANFIELD PLACE 39

CHAPTER V
JOSEPH LACKINGTON 46

CHAPTER VI
A DEPARTURE 55

CHAPTER VII
NORTHERN RELIGION 67

CHAPTER VIII
IN STANSTEAD WOODS 79

CHAPTER IX
THE ALARM 93

CHAPTER X
THE PASSAGE TO THE GARDEN-HOUSE 101

CHAPTER XI
THE GARDEN-HOUSE 113

CHAPTER XII
    THE NIGHT-RIDE 127
CHAPTER XIII
    IN PRISON 132
CHAPTER XIV
    AN OPEN DOOR 145
CHAPTER XV
    THE ROLLING OF THE STONE 156

CHAPTER I
THE COMING OF SPAIN

The conflict between the Old Faith and the lusty young Nation went steadily forward after the Jesuit invasion; more and more priests poured into England; more and more were banished, imprisoned and put to death. The advent of Father Holt, the Jesuit, to Scotland in 1583 was a signal for a new outburst of Catholic feeling, which manifested itself not only in greater devotion to Religion, but, among the ill-instructed and impatient, in very questionable proceedings. In fact, from this time onward the Catholic cause suffered greatly from the division of its supporters into two groups; the religious and the political, as they may be named. The former entirely repudiated any desire or willingness to meddle with civil matters; its members desired to be both Catholics and Englishmen; serving the Pope in matters of Faith and Elizabeth in matters of civil life; but they suffered greatly from the indiscretions and fanaticism of the political group. The members of that party frankly regarded themselves as at war with an usurper and an heretic; and used warlike methods to gain their ends; plots against the Queen's life were set on foot; and their promoters were willing enough to die in defence of the cause. But the civil Government made the fatal mistake of not distinguishing between the two groups; again and again loyal Englishmen were tortured and hanged as traitors, because they shared their faith with conspirators.

There was one question, however, that was indeed on the borderline, exceedingly difficult to answer in words, especially for scrupulous consciences; and that was whether they believed in the Pope's deposing power; and this question was adroitly and deliberately used by the Government in doubtful cases to ensure a conviction. But whether or not it was possible to frame a satisfactory answer in words, yet the accused were plain enough in their deeds; and when the Armada at length was launched in '88, there were no more loyal defenders of England than the persecuted Catholics. Even before this, however, there had appeared signs of reaction among the Protestants, especially against the torture and death of Campion and his fellows; and Lord Burghley in '83 attempted to quiet the people's resentment by his anonymous pamphlet, "Execution of Justice in England," to which Cardinal Allen presently replied.

Ireland, which had been profoundly stirred by the military expedition from the continent in '80, at length was beaten and slashed into submission again; and the torture and execution of Hurley by martial law, which Elizabeth directed on account of his appointment to the See of Cashel, when the judges had pronounced there to be no case against him; and a massacre on the banks of the Moy in '86 of Scots who had come across as reinforcements to the Irish;—these were incidents in the black list of barbarities by which at last a sort of temporary quiet was brought to Ireland.

In Scottish affairs, the tangle, unravelled even still, of which Mary Stuart was the centre, led at last to her death. Walsingham, with extraordinary skill, managed to tempt her into a dangerous correspondence, all of which he tapped on the way: he supplied to her in fact the very instrument—an ingeniously made beer-barrel—through which the correspondence was made possible, and, after reading all the letters, forwarded them to their several destinations. When all was ripe he brought his hand down on a group of zealots, to whose designs Mary was supposed to be privy; and after their execution, finally succeeded, in '87, in obtaining Elizabeth's signature to her cousin's death-warrant. The storm already raging against Elizabeth on the Continent, but fanned to fury by this execution, ultimately broke in the Spanish Armada in the following year.

Meanwhile, at home, the affairs of the Church of England were far from prosperous. Puritanism was rampant; and a wail of dismay was evoked by the new demands of a Commission under Whitgift's guidance, in '82, whereby the Puritan divines were now called upon to assent to the Queen's Supremacy, the Thirty-nine Articles and the Prayer Book. In spite of the opposition, however, of Burghley and the Commons, Whitgift, who had by this time succeeded to Canterbury upon Grindal's death, remained firm; and a long and dreary dispute began, embittered further by the execution of Mr. Copping and Mr. Thacker in '83 for issuing seditious books in the Puritan cause. A characteristic action in this campaign was the issuing of a Puritan manifesto in '84, consisting of a brief, well-written pamphlet of a hundred and fifty pages under the title "A Learned Discourse of Ecclesiastical Government," making the inconsistent claim of desiring a return to the Primitive and Scriptural model, and at the same time of advocating an original scheme, "one not yet handled." It was practically a demand for the Presbyterian system of pastorate and government. To this Dr. Bridges replies with a tremendous tome of over fourteen hundred pages, discharged after three years of laborious toil; and dealing, as the custom then was, line by line, with the Puritan attack. To this in the following year an anonymous

Puritan, under the name of Martin Marprelate, retorts with a brilliant and sparkling riposte addressed to "The right puissant and terrible priests, my clergy-masters of the Convocation-house," in which he mocks bitterly at the prelates, accusing them of Sabbath-breaking, time-serving, and popery,— calling one "dumb and duncetical," another "the veriest coxcomb that ever wore velvet cap," and summing them up generally as "wainscot-faced bishops," "proud, popish, presumptuous, profane paltry, pestilent, and pernicious prelates."

The Archbishop had indeed a difficult team to drive; especially as his coadjutors were not wholly proof against Martin's jibes. In '84 his brother of York had been mixed up in a shocking scandal; in '85 the Bishop of Lichfield was accused of simony; Bishop Aylmer was continually under suspicion of avarice, dishonesty, vanity and swearing; and the Bench as a whole was universally reprobated as covetous, stingy and weak.

In civil matters, England's relation with Spain was her most important concern. Bitter feeling had been growing steadily between the two countries ever since Drake's piracies in the Spanish dominions in America; and a gradually increasing fleet at Cadiz was the outward sign of it. Now the bitterness was deepened by the arrest of English ships in the Spanish ports in the early summer of '85, and the swift reprisals of Drake in the autumn; who intimidated and robbed important towns on the coast, such as Vigo, where his men behaved with revolting irreverence in the churches, and Santiago; and then proceeded to visit and spoil S. Domingo and Carthagena in the Indies.

Again in '87 Drake obtained the leave of the Queen to harass Spain once more, and after robbing and burning all the vessels in Cadiz harbour, he stormed the forts at Faro, destroyed Armada stores at Corunna, and captured the great treasure-ship *San Felipe*.

Elizabeth was no doubt encouraged in her apparent recklessness by the belief that with the Netherlands, which she had been compelled at last to assist, in a state of revolt, Spain would have little energy for reprisals upon England; but she grew more and more uneasy when news continued to arrive in England of the growing preparations for the Armada; France, too, was now so much involved with internal struggles, as the Protestant Henry of Navarre was now the heir to her Catholic throne, that efficacious intervention could no longer be looked for from that quarter, and it seemed at last as if the gigantic Southern power was about to inflict punishment upon the little northern kingdom which had insulted her with impunity so long.

In the October of '87 certain news arrived in England of the gigantic preparations being made in Spain and elsewhere: and hearts began to beat, and tongues to clack, and couriers to gallop. Then as the months went by, and tidings sifted in, there was something very like consternation in the country. Men told one another of the huge armament that was on its way, the vast ships and guns—all bearing down on tiny England, like a bull on a terrier. They spoke of the religious fervour, like that of a crusade, that inspired the invasion, and was bringing the flower of the Spanish nobility against them: the superstitious contrasted their own *Lion, Revenge,* and *Elizabeth Jonas* with the Spanish *San Felipe, San Matteo,* and *Our Lady of the Rosary*: the more practical thought with even deeper gloom of the dismal parsimony of the Queen, who dribbled out stores and powder so reluctantly, and dismissed her seamen at the least hint of delay.

Yet, little by little, as midsummer came and went, beacons were gathering on every hill, ships were approaching efficiency, and troops assembling at Tilbury under the supremely incompetent command of Lord Leicester.

Among the smaller seaports on the south coast, Rye was one of the most active and enthusiastic; the broad shallow bay was alive with fishing-boats, and the steep cobbled streets of the town were filled all day with a chattering exultant crowd, cheering every group of seamen that passed, and that spent long hours at the quay watching the busy life of the ships, and predicting the great things that should fall when the Spaniards encountered the townsfolk, should the Armada survive Drake's onslaught further west.

About July the twentieth more definite news began to arrive. At least once a day a courier dashed in through the south-west gate, with news that all must hold themselves ready to meet the enemy by the end of the month; labour grew more incessant and excitement more feverish.

About six o'clock on the evening of the twenty-ninth, as a long row of powder barrels was in process of shipping down on the quay, the men who were rolling them suddenly stopped and listened; the line of onlookers paused in their comments, and turned round. From the town above came an outburst of cries, followed by the crash of the alarm from the church-tower. In two minutes the quay was empty. Out of every passage that gave on to the main street poured excited men and women, some hysterically laughing, some swearing, some silent and white as they ran. For across the bay westwards, on a point beyond Winchelsea, in the still evening air rose up a stream of smoke shaped like a pine-tree, with a red smouldering root;

and immediately afterwards in answer the Ypres tower behind the town was pouring out a thick drifting cloud that told to the watchers on Folkestone cliffs that the dreaded and longed-for foe was in sight of England.

Then the solemn hours of waiting began to pass. Every day and night there were watchers, straining their eyes westwards in case the Armada should attempt to coast along England to force a landing anywhere, and southwards in case they should pass nearer the French coast on their way to join the Prince of Parma; but there was little to be seen over that wide ring of blue sea except single vessels, or now and again half-a-dozen in company, appearing and fading again on some unknown quest. The couriers that came in daily could not tell them much; only that there had been indecisive engagements; that the Spaniards had not yet attempted a landing anywhere; and that it was supposed that they would not do so until a union with the force in Flanders had been effected.

And so four days of the following week passed; then on Thursday, August the fourth, within an hour or two after sunrise, the solemn booming of guns began far away to the south-west; but the hours passed; and before nightfall all was silent again.

The suspense was terrible; all night long there were groups parading the streets, anxiously conjecturing, now despondently, now cheerfully.

Then once again on the Friday morning a sudden clamour broke out in the town, and almost simultaneously a pinnace slipped out, spreading her wings and making for the open sea. A squadron of English ships had been sighted flying eastwards; and the pinnace was gone to get news. The ships were watched anxiously by thousands of eyes, and boats put out all along the coast to inquire; and within two or three hours the pinnace was back again in Rye harbour, with news that set bells ringing and men shouting. On Wednesday, the skipper reported, there had been an indecisive engagement during the dead calm that had prevailed in the Channel; a couple of Spanish store-vessels had been taken on the following morning, and a general action had followed, which again had been indecisive; but in which the English had hardly suffered at all, while it was supposed that great havoc had been wrought upon the enemy.

But the best of the news was that the Rye contingent was to set sail at once, and unite with the English fleet westward of Calais by mid-day on Saturday. The squadron that had passed was under the command of the

Admiral himself, who was going to Dover for provisions and ammunition, and would return to his fleet before evening.

Before many hours were passed, Rye harbour was almost empty, and hundreds of eyes were watching the ships that carried their husbands and sons and lovers out into the pale summer haze that hung over the coast of France; while a few sharp-eyed old mariners on points of vantage muttered to one another that in the haze there was a patch of white specks to be seen which betokened the presence of some vast fleet.

That night the sun set yellow and stormy, and by morning the cobblestones of Rye were wet and dripping with storm-showers, and a swell was beginning to lap and sob against the harbour walls.

CHAPTER II
MEN OF WAR AND PEACE

The following days passed in terrible suspense for all left behind at Rye. Every morning all the points of vantage were crowded; the Ypres tower itself was never deserted day or night; and all the sharpest eyes in the town were bent continually out over that leaden rolling sea that faded into haze and storm-cloud in the direction of the French coast. But there was nothing to be seen on that waste of waters but the single boats that flew up channel or laboured down it against the squally west wind, far out at sea. Once or twice fishing-boats put in at Rye; but their reports were so contradictory and uncertain that they increased rather than allayed the suspense and misery. Now it was a French boat that reported the destruction of the *Triumph*; now an Englishman that swore to having seen Drake kill Medina-Sidonia with his own hand on his poop; but whatever the news might be, the unrest and excitement ran higher and higher. St. Clare's chapel in the old parish church of St. Nicholas was crowded every morning at five o'clock by an excited congregation of women, who came to beg God's protection on their dear ones struggling out there somewhere towards the dawn with those cruel Southern monsters. Especially great was the crowd on the Tuesday morning following the departure of the ships; for all day on Monday from time to time came a far-off rolling noise from the direction of Calais; which many declared to be thunder, with an angry emphasis that betrayed their real opinion.

When they came out of church that morning, and were streaming down to the quay as usual to see if any news had come in during the night, a seaman called to them from a window that a French vessel was just entering the harbour.

When the women arrived at the water's edge they found a good crowd already assembled on the quay, watching the ship beat in against the north-west wind, which had now set in; but she aroused no particular comment as she was a well-known boat plying between Boulogne and Rye; and by seven o'clock she was made fast to the quay.

There were the usual formalities, stricter than usual during war, to be gone through before the few passengers were allowed to land: but all was in order; the officers left the boat, and the passengers came up the plank, the crowd pressing forward as they came, and questioning them eagerly. No, there was no certain news, said an Englishman at last, who looked like a lawyer; it was said at Boulogne the night before that there had been an engagement further up beyond the Straits; they had all heard guns; and it was reported by the last cruiser who came in before the boat left that a Spanish galleasse had run aground and had been claimed by M. Gourdain, the governor of Calais; but probably, added the shrewd-eyed man, that was just a piece of their dirty French pride. The crowd smiled ruefully; and a French officer of the boat who was standing by the gangway scowled savagely, as the lawyer passed on with a demure face.

Then there was a pause in the little stream of passengers; and then, out of the tiny door that led below decks, walking swiftly, and carrying a long cloak over her arm, came Isabel Norris, in a grey travelling dress, followed by Anthony and a couple of servants. The crowd fell back for the lady, who passed straight up through them; but one or two of the men called out for news to Anthony. He shook his head cheerfully at them.

"I know no more than that gentleman," he said, nodding towards the lawyer; and then followed Isabel; and together they made their way up to the inn.

Anthony was a good deal changed in the last six years; his beard and moustache were well grown; and he had a new look of gravity in his brown eyes; when he had smiled and shaken his head at the eager crowd just now, showing his white regular teeth, he looked as young as ever; but the serious look fell on his face again, as he followed Isabel up the steep little cobbled slope in his buff dress and plumed hat.

There was not so much apparent change in Isabel; she was a shade graver too, her walk a little slower and more dignified, and her lips, a little thinner, had a line of strength in them that was new; and even now as she was treading English ground again for the first time for six years, the look of slight abstraction in her eyes that is often the sign of a strong inner life, was just a touch deeper than it used to be.

They went up together with scarcely a word; and asked for a private room and dinner in two hours' time; and a carriage and horses for the servants to be ready at noon. The landlord, who had met them at the door, shook his head.

"The private room, sir, and the dinner—yes, sir—but the horses——" and he spread his hands out deprecatingly. "There is not one in the stall," he added.

Anthony considered a moment.

"Well, what do you propose? We are willing to stay a day or two, if you think that by then——"

"Ah," said the landlord, "to-morrow is another matter. I expect two of my carriages home to-night, sir, from London; but the horses will not be able to travel till noon to-morrow."

"That will do," said Anthony; and he followed Isabel upstairs.

It was very strange to them both to be back in England after so long. They had settled down at Douai with the Maxwells; but, almost immediately on their arrival, Mistress Margaret was sent for by her Superior to the house of her Order at Brussels; and Lady Maxwell was left alone with Isabel in a house in the town; for Anthony was in the seminary.

Then, in '86 Lady Maxwell had died, quite suddenly. Isabel herself had found her at her prie-dieu in the morning, still in her evening dress; she was leaning partly against the wall; her wrinkled old hands were clasped tightly together on a little ivory crucifix, on the top of the desk; and her snow-white head, with the lace drooping from it like a bridal veil, was bowed below them. Isabel, who had not dared to move her, had sent instantly for a little French doctor, who had thrown up his hands in a kind of devout ecstasy at that wonderful old figure, rigid in an eternal prayer. The two tall tapers she had lighted eight hours before were still just alight beside her, and looked strange in the morning sunshine.

"Pendant ses oraisons! pendant ses oraisons!" he murmured over and over again; and then had fallen on his knees and kissed the drooping lace of her sleeve.

"Priez pour moi, madame," he whispered to the motionless figure.

And so the old Catholic who had suffered so much had gone to her rest. The fact that her son James had been living in the College during her four years' stay at Douai had been perhaps the greatest possible consolation to her for being obliged to be out of England; for she saw him almost daily; and it was he who sang her Requiem. Isabel had then gone to live with other friends in Douai, until Anthony had been ordained priest in the June of '88, and was ready to take her to England; and now the two were bound for Stanfield, where Anthony was to act as chaplain for the present, as Mr. Buxton had predicted so long before. Old Mr. Blake had died in the spring of the year, still disapproving of his patron's liberal notions, and Mr. Buxton had immediately sent a special messenger all the way to Douai to secure Anthony's services; and had insisted moreover that Isabel should accompany her brother. They intended however to call at the Dower House on the way, which had been left under the charge of old Mrs. Carroll; and renew the memories of their own dear home.

They talked little at dinner; and only of general matters, their journey, the Armada, their joy at getting home again; for they had been expressly warned by their friends abroad against any indiscreet talk even when they thought themselves alone, and especially in the seaports, where so constant a watch was kept for seminary priests. The presence of Isabel, however, was the greatest protection to Anthony; as it was almost unknown that a priest should travel with any but male companions.

Then suddenly, as they were ending dinner, a great clamour broke out in the town below them; a gun was fired somewhere; and footsteps began to rush along the narrow street outside. Anthony ran to the window and called to know what was the matter; but no one paid any attention to him; and he presently sat down again in despair, and with one or two wistful looks.

"I will go immediately," he said to Isabel, "and bring you word."

A moment after a servant burst into the room.

"It is a Spanish ship, sir," he said, "a prize—rounding Dungeness."

In the afternoon, when the first fierce excitement was over, Anthony went down to the quay. He did not particularly wish to attract attention, and so he kept himself in the background somewhat; but he had a good view of her as she lay moored just off the quay, especially when one of the town guard who had charge of the ropes that kept the crowd back, seeing a gentleman in the crowd, beckoned him through.

"Your honour will wish to see the prize?" he said, in hopes of a trifle for himself; "make way there for the gentleman."

Anthony thought it better under these circumstances to accept the invitation, so he gave the man something, and slipped through. On the quay was a pile of plunder from the ship: a dozen chests carved and steel-clamped stood together; half-a-dozen barrels of powder; the ship's bell rested amid a heap of rich clothes and hangings; a silver crucifix and a couple of lamps with their chains lay tumbled on one side; and a parson was examining a finely carved mahogany table that stood near.

He looked up at Anthony.

"For the church, sir," he said cheerfully. "I shall make application to her Grace."

Anthony smiled at him.

"A holy revenge, sir," he said.

The ship herself had once been a merchantman brig; so much Anthony could tell, though he knew little of seamanship; but she had been armed heavily with deep bulwarks of timber, pierced for a dozen guns on each broadside. Now, however, she was in a terrible condition. The solid bulwarks were rent and shattered, as indeed was her whole hull; near the waterline were nailed sheets of lead, plainly in order to keep the water from entering the shot-holes; she had only one mast; and that was splintered in more than one place; a spar had been rigged up on to the stump of the bowsprit. The high poop such as distinguished the Spanish vessels was in the same deplorable condition; as well as the figure-head, which represented a beardless man with a halo behind his head, and which bore the marks of fierce hacks as well as of shot.

Anthony read the name,—the *San Juan da Cabellas*.

From the high quay too he could see down on to the middle decks, and there was the most shocking sight of all, for the boards and the mast-stumps and the bulwarks and the ship's furniture were all alike splashed with blood, some of the deeper pools not even yet dry. It was evident that the *San Juan* had not yielded easily.

Presently Anthony saw an officer approaching, and not wishing to be led into conversation slipped away again through the crowd to take Isabel the news.

The two remained quietly upstairs the rest of the afternoon, listening to the singing and the shouting in the streets, and watching from their window the groups that swung and danced to and fro in joy at Rye's contribution to the defeat of the invaders. When the dusk fell the noise was louder than ever as the men began to drink more deep, and torches were continually tossing up and down the steep cobbled streets; the din reached its climax about half-past nine, when the main body of the revellers passed up towards the inn, and, as Anthony saw from the window, finally entered through the archway below; and then all grew tolerably quiet. Presently Isabel said that she would go to bed, but just before she left the room, the servant again came in.

"If you please, sir, Lieutenant Raxham, of the *Seahorse*, is telling the tale of the capture of the Spanish ship; and the landlord bid me come and tell you."

Anthony glanced at Isabel, who nodded at him.

"Yes; go," she said, "and come up and tell me the news afterwards, if it is not very late."

When Anthony came downstairs he found to his annoyance that the place of honour had been reserved for him in a tall chair next to the landlord's at the head of the table. The landlord rose to meet his guest.

"Sit here, sir," he said. "I am glad you have come. And now, Mr. Raxham — —"

Anthony looked about him with some dismay at this extreme publicity. The room was full from end to end. They were chiefly soldiers who sat at the table — heavy-looking rustics from Hawkhurst, Cranbrook and Appledore, in brigantines and steel caps, who had been sent in by the magistrates to the nearest seaport to assist in the defence of the coast — a few of them wore corselets with almain rivets and carried swords, while the pike-heads of the others rose up here and there above the crowd. The rest of the room was filled with the townsmen of Rye — those who had been retained for the defence of the coast, as well as others who for any physical reason could not serve by sea or land. There was an air of extraordinary excitement in the room. The faces of the most stolid were transfigured, for they were gathered to hear of the struggle their own dear England was making; the sickening pause of those months of waiting had ended at last; the huge southern monster had risen up over the edge of the sea, and the panting little country had flown at his throat and grappled him; and now they were hearing the tale of how deep her fangs had sunk.

The crowd laughed and applauded and drew its breath sharply, as one man; and the silence now and then was startling as the young officer told his story; although he had few gifts of rhetoric, except a certain vivid vocabulary. He himself was a lad of eighteen or so, with a pleasant reckless face, now flushed with drink and excitement, and sparkling eyes; he was seated in a chair upon the further end of the table, so that all could hear his story; and he had a cup of huff-cup in his left hand as he talked, leaving his right hand free to emphasise his points and slap his leg in a clumsy sort of oratory. His tale was full of little similes, at which his audience nodded their heads now and then, approvingly. He had apparently already begun his story, for when Anthony had taken his seat and silence had been obtained, he went straight on without any further introduction.

The landlord leaned over to Anthony. "The *San Juan*," he whispered behind his hot hairy hand, and nodded at him with meaning eyes.

"And every time they fired over us," went on the lieutenant, "and we fired into them; and the only damage they did us was their muskets in the tops. They killed Tom Dane like that"—there was a swift hiss of breath from the room; but the officer went straight on—"shot him through the back as he bent over his gun; and wounded old Harry and a score more; but all the while, lads, we were a-pounding at them with the broadsides as we came round, and raking them with the demi-cannon in the poop, until—well; go you and see the craft as she lies at the quay if you would know what we did. I tell you, as we came at her once towards the end, I saw that she was bleeding through her scuppers like a pig, from the middle deck. They were all packed up there together—sailors and soldiers and a priest or two; and scarce a ball could pass between the poop and the forecastle without touching flesh."

The lad stopped a moment and took a pull at his cup, and a murmur of talk broke out in the room. Anthony was surprised at his accent and manner of speaking, and heard afterwards that he was the son of the parson at one of the inland villages, and had had an education. In a moment he went on.

"Well—it would be about noon, just before the Admiral came up from Calais, that the old *Seahorse* was lost. We came at the dons again as we had done before, only closer than ever; and just as the captain gave the word to put her about, a ball from one of their guns which they had trained down on us, cut old Dick Kemp in half at the helm, and broke the tiller to splinters."

"Old Dick?" said a man's voice out of the reeking crowd, "Old Dick?"

There was a murmur round him, bidding him hold his tongue; and the lad went on.

"Well, we drifted nearer and nearer. There was nought to do but to bang at them; and that we did, by God—and to board her if we touched. Well, I worked my saker, and saw little else—for the smoke was like a black sea-fog; and the noise fit to crack your ears. Mine sing yet with it; the captain was bawling from the poop, and there were a dozen pikemen ready below; and then on a sudden came the crash; and I looked up and there was the Spaniards' decks above us, and the poop like a tower, with a grinning don or two looking down; and there was I looking up the muzzle of a culverin. I skipped towards the poop, shouting to the men; and the dons fired their broadside as I went.—God save us from that din! But I knew the old *Seahorse* was done this time—the old ship lurched and shook as the balls tore through her and broke her back; and there was such a yell as you'll never hear this side of hell. Well—I was on the poop by now, and the men after me; for you see the poop of the *Seahorse* was as high as the middle deck of the Spaniard, and we must board from there or not at all. Well, lads, there was the captain before me. He had fought cool till then, as cool as a parson among his roses, with never an oath from his mouth—but now he was as scarlet as a poppy, and his eyes were like blue fire, and his mouth jabbered and foamed; he was so hot, you see, at the loss of his ship. He was dancing to and fro waiting while the poop swung round on the tide; and the old craft plunged deeper in every wave that lifted her, but he cared no more for that nor for the musket-balls from the tops, nor for the brown grinning devils who shook their pikes at him from the decks, than—than a mad dog cares for a shower of leaves; but he stamped there and cursed them and damned them as they laughed at him; and then in a moment the poop touched.

"Well, lads—" and the lieutenant set his cup down on the table, clapped his hands on his knees, laughed shortly and nervously once or twice, and looked round. "Well, lads, I have never seen the like. The captain went for them like a wild cat; one step on the rail and the next among them; and was gone like a stone into water"—and the lad clapped his hand on his thigh. "I saw one face slit up from chin to eye; and another split across like an apple; and then we were after him. The men were mad, too—what was left of us; and we poured up on to the decks and left the old *Seahorse* to die. Well, we had our work before us—but it was no good. The dons could do nothing; I was after the captain as he went through the pack and came out just behind him; there were half a dozen of them down now; and the noise and the foreign oaths went up like smoke; and the captain himself was bleeding down one side of his face and grunting as he cut and stabbed; and I had had a knife through the arm; but he went up on to the poop; and as I followed, the Spaniards broke and threw down their arms—they saw 'twas no use, you see. When we reached the poop-stairs an officer in a blue coat came forward jabbering some jargon; but the captain would have no parley with him, but flung his dag clean into the man's face, and over he went backwards—with his damned high heels in the air."

There was a sudden murmur of laughter from the room; Anthony glanced off the lieutenant's grinning ruddy face for a moment, and saw the rows of listening faces all wrinkled with mirth.

"Well," went on the lad, "up went the captain, and I after him. Then there came across the deck, very slow and stately, the Spanish captain himself, in a fine laced coat and a plumed hat, and he was holding out his sword by the blade and bowed as we ran towards him, and began some damned foreign nonsense, with his *Señor*—but the captain would have none o' that, I tell you he was like Tom o' Bedlam now—so as the Señor grinned at him with his monkey face and bowed and wagged, the captain fetched him a slash across the cheek with his sword that cut up into his head; and that don went spinning across the poop like a morris-man and brought up against the rail, and then down he came," and the lad dashed his hand on his thigh again—"as dead as mutton."

Again came a louder gust of laughter from the room. Anthony half rose in his chair, and then sat down again.

"Well," said the lad, "and that was not all. Down he raged again to the decks and I behind him—I tell you, it was like a butcher's shop—but it was quieter now—the fighting was over—and the Spaniards were all run below, except half-a-dozen in the tops; looking down like young rooks at an archer. There had been a popish priest too with his crucifix in one hand and his god-almighty in the other, over a dying man as we came up; but as we came down there he lay in his black gown with a hole through his heart and his crucifix gone. One of the lads had got it no doubt. Well, the captain brought up at the main mast. 'God's blood,' he bawled, 'where are the brown devils got to?' Some one told him, and pointed down the hatch. Well, then I turned sick with my wound and the smell of the place and all; and I knew nothing more till I found myself sitting on a dead don, with the captain holding me up and pouring a cordial down my throat."

Then talk and laughter broke out in the audience; but the landlord held up his hand for silence.

"And what of the others?" he shouted.

"Dead meat too," said the lad—"the captain went down with a dozen or more and hunted them out and finished them. There was one, Dick told me afterwards," and the lieutenant gave a cackle of mirth, "that they hunted twice round the ship before he jumped over yelling to some popish saint to help him; but it seems he was deaf, like the old Baal that parson tells of o' Sundays. The dirty swine to run like that! Well, he's got his bellyful now of the salt water that he came so far to see. And then the captain with his own hands trained a robinet that was on the poop on to the tops; and down the birds came, one by one; for their powder up there was all shot off."

"And the *Seahorse*?" said the landlord again.

There fell a dead silence: all in the room knew that the ship was lost, but it was terrible to hear it again. The lad's face broke into lines of grief, and he spoke huskily.

"Gone down with the dead and wounded; and the rest of the fleet a mile away."

Then the lieutenant went on to describe how he himself had been deputed to bring the *San Juan* into port with the wounded on board, while the captain and the rest of the crew by Drake's orders attached themselves to various vessels that were short-handed, and how the English fleet had followed what was left of the Spaniards when the fight ended at sunset, up towards the North Sea.

When he finished his story there was a tremendous outburst of cheering and hammering upon the table, and the feet and the pike-butts thundered on the floor, and a name was cried again and again as the cups were emptied.

"God save her Grace and old England!" yelled a slim smooth-faced archer from Appledore.

"God send the dons and all her foes to hell!" roared a burly pikeman with his cup in the air. Then the room shook again as the toasts were drunk with applauding feet and hands.

Anthony turned to the landlord, who had just ceased thumping with his great red fists on the table.

"What was the captain's name?" he asked, when a slight lull came.

"Maxwell," said the crimson-faced man. "Hubert Maxwell—one of Drake's own men."

When Anthony came upstairs he heard his name called through the door, and went in to Isabel's room to find her sitting up in bed in the gloom of the summer night; the party below had broken up, and all was quiet except for the far-off shouts and hoots of cheerful laughter from the dispersing groups down among the narrow streets.

"Well?" she said, as he came in and stood in the doorway.

"It is just the story of the prize," he said, "and it seems that Hubert had the taking of it."

There was silence a moment. Anthony could see her face, a motionless pale outline, and her arms clasped round her knees as she sat up in bed.

"Hubert?" she asked in an even voice.

"Yes, Hubert."

There was silence a moment.

"Well?" she said again.

"He is safe," said Anthony, "and fought gallantly. I will tell you more to-morrow."

"Ah!" said Isabel softly; and then lay down again.

"Good-night, Anthony."

"Good-night."

But Anthony dared not tell her the details next day, after all.

There was still a difficulty about the horses; they had not arrived until the Wednesday morning, and were greatly exhausted by a long and troublesome journey; so the travellers consented to postpone their journey for yet one more day. The weather, which had been thickening, grew heavier still in the afternoon, and great banks of clouds were rising out of the west. Anthony started out about four o'clock for a walk along the coast; and, making a long round in the direction of Lydd, did not finally return until about seven. As he came in at the north-east of the town he noticed how empty the streets were, and passed on down in the direction of the quay. As he turned down the steep street into the harbour groups began to pour up past him, laughing and exclaiming; and in a moment more came Isabel walking alone. He looked at her anxiously, for he saw something had happened. Her quiet face was lit up with some interior emotion, and her mouth was trembling.

"The Armada is routed," she said; "and I have seen Hubert."

The two turned back together and walked silently up to the inn. There she told him the story. She had been told that Captain Maxwell was come in the *Elizabeth*, for provisions for Lord Howard Seymour's squadron, to which his new command was attached; and that he was even now in harbour. At that she had gone straight down alone.

"Oh, Anthony!" she cried, "you know how it is with me. I could not help it. I am not ashamed of it. God Almighty knows all, and is not wrath with me. So I went down and was in the crowd as he came down again with the mayor, Mr. Hamon; we all made way for them, and the men cheered themselves scarlet; but he came down cool and quiet; you know his way—with his eyes half shut; and—and—he was so brown; and he looks sad—and he had a great plaister on the left temple. And then he saw me."

Isabel sprang up, and came up to Anthony and took his hands. "Oh! Anthony; I was very happy then; because he took off his cap and bowed; and his face was all lighted; and he took my hand and kissed it—and then made Mr. Hamon known to me. The crowd laughed and said things—but I did not care; and he soon silenced them, he looked round so fiercely; and then I went on board with him—he would have it so—and he showed us everything—and we sat a little in the cabin; and he told me of his wife and child. She is the daughter of a Plymouth minister; he knew her when he was with Drake; and he told me all about her, so you see——" Isabel broke off; and sat down in the high window seat. "And then he asked me about you; and I said you were here; and that we were going to stay a little while with Mr. Buxton of Stanfield—you see I knew we could trust him; and Mr.

Hamon was in the passage just then looking at the guns; and then a sailor came in to say that all was ready; and so we came away. But it was so good to see him again; and to know that he was so happy."

Anthony looked at his sister in astonishment; her quiet manner was gone, and she was talking again almost like an excited child; and so happily. It was very strange, he thought. He sat down beside her.

"Oh, Anthony!" she said, "do you understand? I love him dearly still; and his wife and child too. God bless them all and keep them!"

The mystery was still deep to him; and he feared to say what he should not; so he kissed Isabel silently; and the two sat there together and looked out over the crowding red roofs to the glowing western sky across the bay below them.

CHAPTER III
HOME-COMING

It was a stormy summer evening as the brother and sister rode up between the last long hills that led to Great Keynes. A south-west wind had been rising all day, that same wind that was now driving the ruined Armada up into the fierce North Sea, with the fiercer men behind to bar the return. But here, twenty miles inland, with the high south-downs to break the gale, the riders were in comparative quiet, though the great trees overhead tossed their heavy rustling heads as the gusts struck them now and again.

The party had turned off, as the dusk was falling, from the main-road into bridle-paths that they knew well, and were now approaching the village through the water meadows on the south-east side along a ride that would bring them, round the village, direct to the Dower House. In the gloom Anthony could make out the tall reeds, and the loosestrife and willowherb against them, that marked the course of the stream where he had caught trout, as a boy; and against the western sky, as he turned in his saddle, rose up the high windy hills where he had hawked with Hubert so many years before. It was a strange thought to him as he rode along that his very presence here in his own country was an act of high treason by the law lately passed, and that every day he lived here must be a day of danger.

For Isabel, too, it was strange to be riding up again towards the battlefield of her desires—that battlefield where she had lived for years in such childish faith and peace without a suspicion of the forces that were lurking beneath her own quiet nature. But to both of them the sense of home-coming was stronger than all else—that strange passion for a particular set of inanimate things—or, at the most, for an association of ideas—that has no parallel in human emotions; and as they rode up the darkening valley and the lights of the high windows of the Hall began to show over the trees on their right, Anthony forgot his treason and Isabel her conflicts, and both felt a lump rise in the throat, and their hearts begin to beat quicker with a strange pleasurable pulse, and to Isabel's eyes at least there rose up great tears of happiness and content; neither dared speak, but both looked eagerly about at the pool where the Mayflies used to dance, at the knoll where the pigeons nested, at the little low bridge beneath which their inch-long boats used to slide sideways into darkness, and the broad marshy flats where the gorgeous irises grew.

"How the trees have grown!" said Anthony at last, with an effort; "I cannot see the lights from the house."

"Mrs. Carroll will have made ready the first-floor rooms then, on the south."

"I am sorry they are not our own," said Anthony.

"Ah, look! there is the dovecote," cried Isabel.

They were passing up now behind the farm buildings; and directly afterwards came round in front of the little walled garden to the west of the house.

There was a sudden exclamation from Anthony; and Isabel stared in silent dismay. The old house rose up before them with its rows of square windows against the night sky, dark. There was not a glimmer anywhere; even Mrs. Carroll's own room on the south was dark. They reined their horses in and stood a moment.

"Oh, Anthony, Anthony!" cried Isabel suddenly, "what is it? Is there no one there?"

Anthony shook his head; and then put his tired beast to a shambling trot with Isabel silent again with weariness and disappointment behind him. They passed along outside the low wall, turned the corner of the house and drew up at the odd little doorway in the angle at the back of the house. The servants had drawn up behind them, and now pressed up to hold their horses; and the brother and sister slipped off and went towards the door. Anthony passed under the little open porch and put his hand out to the door; it was quite dark underneath the porch, and he felt further and further, and yet there was no door; his foot struck the step. He felt his way to the doorposts and groped for the door; but still there was none; he could feel the panelling of the lobby inside the doorway, and that was all. He drew back, as one would draw back from a dead face on which one had laid a hand in the dark.

"Oh, Anthony!" said Isabel again, "what is it?" She was still outside.

"Have you a light?" said Anthony hoarsely to the servants.

The man nearest him bent and fumbled in the saddle-bags, and after what seemed an interminable while kindled a little bent taper and handed it to him. As he went towards the porch shading it with his hand, Isabel sprang past him and went before; and then, as the light fell through the doorway, stopped in dead and bewildered silence.

The door was lying on the floor within, shattered and splintered.

Anthony stepped beside her, and she turned and clung to his arm, and a sob or two made itself heard. Then they looked about them. The banisters above them were smashed, and like a cataract, down the stairs lay a confused heap of crockery, torn embroidery and clothes, books, and broken furniture.

Anthony's hand shook so much that the shadows of the broken banisters waved on the wall above like thin exulting dancers.

Suddenly Anthony started.

"Mrs. Carroll," he exclaimed, and he darted upstairs past the ruins into her two rooms halfway up the flight; and in a minute or two was back with Isabel.

"She has escaped," he said in a low voice; and then the two stood looking about them silently again. The door leading to the cellars on the left was broken too; and fragments of casks and bottles lay about the steps; the white wall was splashed with drink, and there was a smell of spirits in the air. Evidently the stormers had thought themselves worthy of their hire.

"Come," he said again; and leaving the entrance lobby, the two passed to the hall-door and pushed that open and looked. There was the same furious confusion there; the tapestry was lying tumbled and rent on the floor—the high oak mantelpiece was shattered, and doleful cracks and splinters in the panelling all round showed how mad the attack had been; one of the pillars of the further archway was broken clean off, and the brickwork showed behind; the pictures had been smashed and added to the heap of wrecked furniture and broken glass in the middle.

"Come," he said once more; and the two passed silently through the broken archway, and going up the other flight of stairs, gradually made the round of the house. Everywhere it was the same, except in the servants' attics, where, apparently, the mob had not thought it worth while to go.

Isabel's own room was the most pitiable of all; the windows had only the leaden frames left, and those bent and battered; the delicate panelling was scarred and split by the shower of stones that had poured in through the window and that now lay in all parts of the room. A painting of her mother that had hung over her bed was now lying face downwards on the floor. Isabel turned it over silently; a stone had gone through the face; and it had been apparently slit too by some sharp instrument. Even the slender oak bed was smashed in the centre, as if half a dozen men had jumped upon it at once; and the little prie-dieu near the window had been deliberately hacked in half. Isabel looked at it all with wide startled eyes and parted lips;

and then suddenly sank down on the wrecked bed where she had hoped to sleep that night, and began to sob like a child.

"Ah! I did think—I did think——" she began.

Anthony stooped and tried to lift her.

"Come, my darling," he said, "is not this a high honour? *Qui relinquit domos!*"

"Oh! why have they done it?" sobbed Isabel. "What harm have we done them?" and she began to wail. She was thoroughly over-tired and over-wrought; and Anthony could not find it in his heart to blame her; but he spoke again bravely.

"We are Catholics," he said; "that is why they have done it. Do not throw away this grace that our Lord has given us; embrace it and make it yours."

It was the priest that was speaking now; and Isabel turned her face and looked at him; and then got up and hid her face on his shoulder.

"Oh, Anthony, help me!" she said; and so stood there, quiet.

He came down presently to the servants, while Isabel went upstairs to prepare the rooms in the attics; for it was impossible for them to ride further that night; so they settled to sleep there, and stable the horses; and to ride on early the next day, and be out of the village before the folks were about. Anthony gave directions to the servants, who were Catholics too, and explained in a word or two what had happened; and bade them come up to the house as soon as they had fed and watered the beasts; meanwhile he took the saddle-bags indoors and spread out their remaining provisions in one of the downstairs rooms; and soon Isabel joined him.

"I have made up five beds," she said, and her voice and lips were steady, and her eyes grave and serene again.

The five supped together in the wrecked kitchen, a fine room on the east of the house, supported by a great oak pillar to which the horses of guests were sometimes attached when the stable was full.

Isabel managed to make a fire and to boil some soup; but they hung thick curtains across the shattered windows, and quenched the fire as soon as the soup was made, for fear that either the light or the smoke from the chimney should arouse attention.

When supper was over, and the two men-servants and Isabel's French maid were washing up in the scullery, Isabel suddenly turned to Anthony as they sat together near the fireplace.

"I had forgotten," she said, "what we arranged as we rode up. I must go and tell her still."

Anthony looked at her steadily a moment.

"God keep you," he said.

She kissed him and took her riding-cloak, drew the hood over her head, and went out into the dark.

It was with the keenest relief that, half an hour later, Anthony heard her footstep again in the red-tiled hall outside. The servants were gone upstairs by now, and the house was quiet. She came in, and sat by him again and took his hand.

"Thank God I went," she said. "I have left her so happy."

"Tell me all," said Anthony.

"I went through the garden," said Isabel, "but came round to the front of the house so that they might not think I came from here. When the servant came to the door—he was a stranger, and a Protestant no doubt—I said at once that I brought news of Mr. Maxwell from Rye; and he took me straight in and asked me to come in while he fetched her woman. Then her woman came out and took me upstairs, up into Lady Maxwell's old room; and there she was lying in bed under the great canopy. Oh, Anthony, she is so pretty! her golden hair was lying out all over the pillow, and her face is so sweet. She cried out when I came in, and lifted herself on her elbow; so I just said at once, 'He is safe and well'; and then she went off into sobs and laughter; so that I had to go and soothe her—her woman was so foolish and helpless; and very soon she was quiet: and then she called me her darling, and she kissed me again and again; and told the woman to go and leave us together; and then she lifted the sheet; and showed me the face of a little child. Oh Anthony; Hubert's child and hers, the second, born on Tuesday—only think of that. 'Mercy, I was going to call her,' she said, 'if I had not heard by to-morrow, but now I shall call her Victory.'"

Anthony looked quickly at his sister, with a faint smile in his eyes.

"And what did you say?" he asked.

Isabel smiled outright; but her eyes were bright with tears too.

"'You have guessed,' she said. 'Yes,' I said, 'call her Mercy all the same,' and she kissed me again, and cried, and said that she would. And then I told her all about Hubert; and about his little wound; and how well he looked; and how all the fighting was most likely over; and what his cabin looked like. And then she suddenly guessed who I was, and asked me; and I could not deny it, you know; but she promised not to tell. Then she told me all about the house here; and how she was afraid Hubert had said something impatient about people who go to foreign parts and leave their country to be attacked, 'But you know he did not really mean it,' she said; and of course he did not. Well, the people had remembered that, and it spread and spread; and when the news of the Armada came last week, a mob came over from East Grinsted, and they sat drinking and drinking in the village; and of course Grace could not go out to them; and all the old people are gone, and the Catholics on the estate—and so at last they all came out roaring and shouting down the drive, and Mrs. Carroll was warned and slipped out to the Hall; and she is now gone to Stanfield to wait for us—and then the crowd broke into the house—but, oh Anthony, Grace was so sorry, and cried sore to think of us here; and asked us to come and stay there; but of course I told her we could not: and then I said a prayer for her; and we kissed one another again; and then I came away."

Anthony looked at his sister, and there was honour and pride of her in his eyes.

The ride to Stanfield next day was a long affair, at a foot's-pace all the way: the horses were thoroughly tired with their journey, and they were obliged to start soon after three o'clock in the morning after a very insufficient rest; they did not reach Groombridge till nearly ten o'clock, when they dined, and then rode on towards Tonbridge about noon. There were heavy hearts to be carried as well. The attempt to welcome the misery of their home-coming was a bitter effort; all the more bitter for that it was an entirely unexpected call upon them. During those six years abroad probably not a day had passed without visions of Great Keynes, and the pleasant and familiar rooms and garden of their own house, and mental rehearsals of their return. The shock of the night before too had been emphasised by the horror of the cold morning light creeping through the empty windows on to the cruel heaps within. The garden too, seen in the dim morning, with its trampled lawns and wrecked flower-beds heaped with withered sunflowers, bell-blossoms and all the rich August growth, with the earthen flower-bowls smashed, the stone balls on the gate overturned, and the laurels at the corner uprooted—all this was a horrible pain to Isabel, to whom the garden was very near as dear and familiar as her own room. So it was a silent and sorrowful ride; and Anthony's heart rose in relief as at last up the grey village-street he saw the crowded roofs of Stanfield Place rise over the churchyard wall.

Their welcome from Mr. Buxton went far to compensate for all.

"My dear boy," he said, "or, my dear father, as I should call you in private, you do not know what happiness is mine to-day. It is a great thing to have a priest again; but, if you will allow me to say so, it is a greater to have my friend—and what a sister you have upstairs!"

They were in Mr. Buxton's own little room on the ground-floor, and Isabel had gone to rest until supper.

Anthony told him of the grim surprise that had awaited them at Great Keynes. "So you must forgive my sister if she is a little sad."

"Yes, yes," said Mr. Buxton, "I had heard from Mrs. Carroll last night when she arrived here. But there was no time to warn you. I had expected you to-day, though Mrs. Carroll did not."

(Anthony had sent a man straight from Rye to Stanfield.)

"But Mistress Isabel, as I shall venture to call her, must do what she can with this house and garden. I need not say how wholly it is hers. And I shall call you Anthony," he added—"in public, at least. And, for strangers, you are just here as my guest; and you shall be called Capell—a sound name; and you shall be Catholics too; though you are no priest, of course, in public—and you have returned from the Continent. I hold it is no use to lie when you can be found out. I do not know what your conscience is, Father Anthony; but, for myself, I count us Catholics to be *in statu belli* now; and therefore I shall lie frankly and fully when there is need; and you may do as you please. Old Mr. Blake used to bid me prevaricate instead; but that always seemed to me two lies instead of one—one to the questioning party and the other to myself; and so I always said to him, but he would not have it so. I wondered he did not tell me that two negatives made an affirmative; but he was not clever enough, the good father. So my own custom is to tell one plain lie when needed, and shame the devil."

It was pleasant to Anthony to hear his friend talk again, and he said so. His host's face softened into a great tenderness.

"Dear lad, I know what you mean. Please God you may find this a happy home."

A couple of hours later, when Anthony and Isabel came down together from their rooms in the old wing, they found Mr. Buxton in his black satin and lace in the beautiful withdrawing-room on the ground-floor. It was already past the supper-hour, but their host showed no signs of going into the hall. At last he apologised.

"I ask your pardon, Mistress Isabel; but I have a guest come to stay with me, who only arrived an hour ago; and she is a great lady and must have her time. Ah! here she is."

The door was flung open and a radiant vision appeared. The door was a little way off, and there were no candles near it; but there swelled and rustled into the room a figure all in blue and gold, with a white delicate ruff; and diamond buckles shone beneath the rich brocaded petticoat. Above rose a white bosom and throat scintillating with diamonds, and a flushed face with scarlet lips, all crowned by piles of black hair, with black dancing eyes beneath. Still a little in the shadow this splendid figure swept down with a great curtsey, which Isabel met by another, while the two gentlemen bowed low; and then, as the stranger swayed up again into the full light of the sconces, Anthony recognised Mary Corbet.

He stood irresolute with happy hesitation; and she came up smiling brilliantly; and before he could stay her dropped down on one knee and took his hand and kissed it; just as the man left the room.

"God bless you, Father Anthony!" she said; and as he looked at her, as she glanced up, he could not tell whether her eyes shone with tears or laughter.

"This is very charming and proper, Mistress Corbet, and like a true daughter of the Church," put in Mr. Buxton, "but I shall be obliged to you if you will not in future kiss priests' hands nor call them Father in the presence of the servants—at least not in my house."

"Ah!" she said, "you were always prudent. Have you seen his secret doors?" she went on to Anthony. "The entire Catholic Church might play hare and hounds with the Holy Father as huntsman and the Cardinals as the whips, through Mr. Buxton's secret labyrinths."

"Wait until you are hare, and it is other than Holy Church that is a-hunting," said Mr. Buxton, "and you will thank God for my labyrinths, as you call them."

Then she greeted Isabel with great warmth.

"Why, my dear," she said, "you are not the little Puritan maiden any longer. We must have a long talk to-night; and you shall tell me everything."

"Mistress Mary is not so greatly changed," said Isabel, smiling. "She always would be told everything."

It was strange to Anthony to meet Mary again after so long, and to find her so little changed, as Isabel had said truly. He himself had passed through so much since they had last met at Greenwich over six years ago—his conversion, his foreign sojourn, and, above all, the bewildering and intoxicating sweetness of his ordination and priestly life. And yet he felt as close to Mary as ever, knit in a bond of wonderful good fellowship and brotherhood such as he had never felt to any other in just that kind and degree. He watched her, warm and content, as she talked across the polished oak and beneath the gleam of the candles; and listened, charmed by her air and her talk.

"There is not so much news of her Grace," she said, "save that she is turning soldier in her old age. She rode out to Tilbury, you know, the other day, in steel cuirass and scarlet; out to see her dear Robin and the army; and her royal face was all smiles and becks, and lord! how the soldiers cheered! But if you had seen her as I did, in her room when she first buckled on her armour, and the joints did not fit—yes, and heard her! there were no smiles to spare then. She lodged at Mr. Rich's, you know, two nights; but he would be Mr. Poor, I should suppose, by the time her Grace left him; for he will not see the worth of a shoelace again of all that he expended on her."

"You see," remarked Mr. Buxton to Isabel, "how fortunate we are in having such a friend of her Grace's with us. We hear all the cream of the news, even though it be a trifle sour sometimes."

"A lover of her Grace," said Mary, "loves the truth about her, however bitter. But then I have no secret passages where I may hide from my sovereign!"

"The cream can scarce be but sour," said Anthony, "near her Grace: there is so much thunder in the air."

"Yes, but the sun came out when you were there, Anthony," put in Isabel, smiling.

"But even the light of her glorious countenance is trying," said Mary. "She is overpowering in thunder and sunshine alike."

"We have had enough of that metaphor," observed Mr. Buxton.

Then Anthony had to talk, and tell all the foreign news of Douai and Rome and Cardinal Allen; and of Father Persons' scheme for a college at Valladolid.

"Father Robert is a superb beggar—as he is superb in all things," said Mr. Buxton. "I dare not think how much he got from me for his college; and then I do not even approve of his college. His principles are too logical for me. I have ever had a weakness for the *non sequitur*."

This led on to the Armada; Anthony told his experience of it; how he had seen at least the sails of Lord Howard's squadron far away against the dawn; and this led on again to a sharp discussion when the servants had left the room.

"I do not know," said Mary at last; "it is difficult—is not the choice between God and Elizabeth? If I were a man, why should I not take up arms to defend my religion? Since I am a woman, why should I not pray for Philip's success? It is a bitter hard choice, I know; but why need I prefer my country to my faith? Tell me that, Father Anthony."

"I can only tell you my private opinion," said Anthony, "and that is, that both duties may be done. As Mr. Buxton here used to tell me, the duty to Cæsar is as real as the duty to God. A man is bound to both; for each has its proper bounds. When either oversteps them it must be resisted. When Elizabeth bids me deny my faith, I tell her I would sooner die. When a priest bids me deny my country, I tell him I would sooner be damned."

Mary clapped her hands.

"I like to hear a man talk like that," she cried. "But what of the Holy Father and his excommunication of her Grace?"

Anthony looked up at her sharply, and then smiled; Isabel watched him with a troubled face.

"Aquinas holds," he said, "that an excommunication of sovereign and people in a lump is invalid. And until the Holy Father tells me himself that Aquinas is wrong, I shall continue to think he is right."

"God-a-mercy!" burst in Mr. Buxton, "what a to-do! Leave it alone until the choice must be made; and meanwhile say your prayers for Pope and Queen too, and hear mass and tell your beads and hold your tongue: that is what I say to myself. Mistress Mary, I will not have my chaplain heckled; here is his lady sister all a-tremble between heresy and treason."

They sat long over the supper-table, talking over the last six years and the times generally. More than once Mary showed a strange bitterness against the Queen. At last Mr. Buxton showed his astonishment plainly.

"I do not understand you," he said. "I know that at heart you are loyal; and yet one might say you meditated her murder."

Mary's face grew white with passion and her eyes blazed.

"Ah!" she hissed, "you do not understand, you say? Then where is your heart? But then you did not see Mary Stuart die."

Anthony looked at her, amazed.

"And you did, Mistress Mary?" he asked.

Mary bowed, with her lips set tight to check their trembling.

"I will tell you," she said, "if our host permits"; and she glanced at him.

"Then come this way," he said, and they rose from table.

They went back again to the withdrawing-room; a little cedar-fire had been kindled under the wide chimney; and the room was full of dancing shadows. The great plaster-pendants, the roses, the crowns, and the portcullises on the ceiling seemed to waver in the firelight, for Mr. Buxton at a sign from Mary blew out the four tapers that were burning in the sconces. They all sat down in the chairs that were set round the fire, Mary in a tall porter's chair with flaps that threw a shadow on her face when she leaned back; and she took a fan in her hand to keep the fire, or her friends' eyes, from her face should she need it.

She first told them very briefly of the last months of Mary's life, of the web that was spun round her by Walsingham's tactics, and her own friends' efforts, until it was difficult for her to stir hand or foot without treason, real or pretended, being set in motion somewhere. Then she described how at Christmas '86 Elizabeth had sent her—Mary Corbet—as a Catholic, up to the Queen of the Scots at Fotheringay, on a private mission to attempt to win the prisoner's confidence, and to persuade her to confess to having been privy to Babington's conspiracy; and how the Scottish Queen had utterly denied it, even in the most intimate conversations. Sentence had been already passed, but the warrant had not been signed; and it never would have been signed, said Mistress Corbet, if Mary had owned to the crime of which she was accused.

"Ah! how they insulted her!" cried Mary Corbet indignantly. "She showed me one day the room where her throne had stood. Now the cloth of state had been torn down by Sir Amyas Paulet's men, and he himself dared to sit with his hat on his head in the sovereign's presence! The insolence of the hound! But the Queen showed me how she had hung a crucifix where her royal arms used to hang. 'J'appelle,' she said to me, 'de la reine au roi des rois.'"

Mistress Corbet went on to tell of the arrival of Walsingham's brother-in-law, Mr. Beale, with the death-warrant on that February Sunday evening.

"I saw his foxy face look sideways up at the windows as he got off his horse in the courtyard; and I knew that our foes had triumphed. Then the other bloodhounds began to arrive; my lord of Kent on the Monday and Shrewsbury on the Tuesday. Then they came in to us after dinner; and they told her Grace it was to be for next day. I was behind her chair and saw her hand on the boss of the arm, and it did not stir nor clench; she said it could not be. She could not believe it of Elizabeth.

"When she did at last believe it, there was no wild weeping or crying for mercy; but she set her affairs in order, queenly, and yet sedately too. She first thought of her soul, and desired that M. de Preau might come to her and hear her confession; but they would not permit it. They offered her Dr. Fletcher instead, 'a godly man,' as my lord of Kent called him. 'Je ne m'en doute pas,' she said, smiling. But it was hard not to have a priest.

"Then she set her earthly affairs in order when she had examined her soul and made confession to God without the Dean's assistance. We all supped together when it was growing late; and I thought, Father Anthony—indeed I did—of another Supper long ago. Then M. Gorion was sent for to arrange some messages and gifts; and until two of the clock in the morning we watched with her or served her as she wrote and gave orders. The court outside was full of comings and goings. As I passed down the passage I saw the torches of the visitors that were come to see the end; and once I heard a hammering from the great hall. Then she went to her bed; and I think few lay as quiet as she in the castle that night. I was with her ladies when they waked her before dawn; and it was hard to see that sweet face on the pillow open its eyes again to what was before her.

"Then when she was dressed I went in again, and we all went to the oratory, where she received our Saviour from the golden pyx which the Holy Father had sent her; for, you see, they would allow no priest to come near her....

"Presently the gentlemen knocked. When we tried to follow we were prevented; they wished her to die alone among her enemies; but at last two of the ladies were allowed to go with her.

"I ran out another way, and sent a message to my Lord Shrewsbury, who knew me at court. As I waited in the courtyard, the musicians there were playing 'The Witches' Dirge,' as is done at the burnings—and all to mock at my queen! At last a halberdier was sent to bring me in."

Mary Corbet was silent a moment or two and leaned back in her chair; and the others dared not speak. The strange emotion of her voice and the stillness of that sparkling figure in the porter's chair affected them profoundly. Her face was now completely shaded by a fan.

"It was in the hall, where a great fire was burning on the hearth. The stage stood at the upper end; all was black. The crowd of gentlemen filled the hall and all were still and reverent except—except a devil who laughed as my queen came in, all in black. She was smiling and brave, and went up the steps and sat on her black throne and looked about her. The—the *things* were just in front of her.

"Then the warrant was read by Beale, and I saw the lords glance at her as it ended; but there was nought but joyous hope in her face. She looked now and again gently on the ivory crucifix in her hand, as she listened; and her lips moved to—to—Him who was delivered to death for her."

Mary Corbet gave one quick sob, and was silent again for an instant. Then she went on in a yet lower voice.

"Dr. Fletcher tried to address her, but he stammered and paused three or four times; and the queen smiled on him and bade him not trouble himself, for that she lived and died a Catholic. But they would not let her be; so she looked on her crucifix and was silent; and even then my lord of Kent badgered her and told her Christ crucified in her hand would not save her, except He was engraved on her heart.

"Then she knelt at her chair and tried to pray softly to herself; but Fletcher would not have that, and prayed himself, aloud, and all the gentlemen in the hall began to pray aloud with him. But Mary prayed on in Latin and English aloud, and prevailed, for all were silent at the end but she.

"And at last she kissed the crucifix and cried in a sweet piercing voice, 'As thine arms, O Jesus, were spread upon the Cross, so receive me into Thy mercy and forgive me my sins!'"

Again Mistress Corbet was silent; and Anthony drew a long sobbing breath of pure pity, and Isabel was crying quietly to herself.

"When the headsmen offered to assist her," went on the low voice, "the queen smiled at the gentlemen and said that she had never had such grooms before; and then they let the ladies come up. When they began to help her with her dress I covered my face—I could not help it. There was such a stillness now that I could hear her beads chink at her girdle. When I looked again, she was ready, with her sweet neck uncovered: all round her was black but the headsman, who wore a white apron over his velvet, and she, in her beauty, and oh! her face was so fair and delicate and her eyes so tender and joyous. And as her ladies looked at her, they sobbed piteously. 'Ne criez vous,' said she.

"Then she knelt down, and Mistress Mowbray bound her eyes. She smiled again under the handkerchief. 'Adieu,' she said, and then, 'Au revoir.'

"Then she said once more a Latin psalm, and then laid her head down, as on a pillow.

"'In manus tuas, Domine,' she said."

Mary Corbet stopped, and leaned forward a little, putting her hand into her bosom; Anthony looked at her as she drew up a thin silk cord with a ruby ring attached to it.

"This was hers," she said simply, and held it out. Each of the Catholics took it and kissed it reverently, and Mary replaced it.

"When they lifted her," she added, "a little dog sprang out from her clothes and yelped. And at that the man near me, who had laughed as she came in, wept."

Then the four sat silent in the firelight.

CHAPTER IV
STANFIELD PLACE

Life at Stanfield Place was wonderfully sweet to Anthony and Isabel after their exile abroad, for both of them had an intense love of England and of English ways. The very sight of fair-faced children, and the noise of their shrill familiar voices from the village street, the depths of the August woods round them, the English manners of living—all this was alive with a full deliberate joy to these two. Besides, there was the unfailing tenderness and gaiety of Mr. Buxton; and at first there was the pleasant company of Mary Corbet as well.

There was little or no anxiety resting on any of them. "God was served," as the celebration of mass was called, each morning in the little room where Anthony had made the exercises, and the three others were always present. It was seldom that the room was not filled to over-flowing on Sundays and holy-days with the household and the neighbouring Catholics.

Everything was, of course, perfection in the little chapel when it was furnished; as was all that Mr. Buxton possessed. There was a wonderful golden crucifix by an unknown artist, that he had picked up in his travels, that stood upon the altar, with the bird-types of the Saviour at each of the four ends; a pelican at the top, an eagle on the right supporting its young which were raising their wings for a flight, on the left a phœnix amid flames, and at the foot a hen gathering her chickens under her wings—all the birds had tiny emerald eyes; the figure on the cross was beautifully wrought, and had rubies in hands and feet and side. There were also two silver altar-candlesticks designed by Marrina for the Piccolomini chapel in the church of St. Francis in Siena; and two more, plainer, for the Elevation. The vestments were exquisite; those for high festivals were cloth of gold; and the other white ones were beautifully worked with seed pearls, and jewelled crosses on the stole and maniple. The other colours, too, were well represented, and were the work of a famous convent in the south of France. All the other articles, too, were of silver: the lavabo basin, the bell, the thurible, the boat and spoon, and the cruets. It was a joy to all the Catholics who came to see the worship of God carried on with such splendour, when in so many places even necessaries were scarcely forthcoming.

There was a little hiding-hole between the chapel and the priest's room, just of a size to hold the altar furniture and the priests in case of a sudden alarm; and there were several others in the house too, which Mr. Buxton had showed to Anthony with a good deal of satisfaction, on the morning after his arrival.

"I dared not show them to you the last time you were here," he said, "and there was no need; but now there must be no delay. I have lately made some more, too. Now here is one," he said, stopping before the great carved mantelpiece in the hall.

He looked round to see that no servant was in the room, and then, standing on a settee before the fire, touched something above, and a circular hole large enough for a man to clamber through appeared in the midst of the tracery.

"There," he said, "and you will find some cured ham and a candle, with a few dates within, should you ever have need to step up there—which, pray God, you may not."

"What is the secret?" asked Anthony, as the tracery swung back into place, and his host stepped down.

"Pull the third roebuck's ears in the coat of arms, or rather push them. It closes with a spring, and is provided with a bolt. But I do not recommend that refuge unless it is necessary. In winter it is too hot, for the chimney passes behind it; and in summer it is too oppressive, for there is not too much air."

At the end of the corridor that led in the direction of the little old rooms where Anthony had slept in his visit, Mr. Buxton stopped before the portrait of a kindly-looking old gentleman that hung on the wall.

"Now there is an upright old man you would say; and indeed he was, for he was my own uncle, and made a godly end of it last year. But now see what a liar I have made of him!"

Mr. Buxton put his hand behind the frame, and the whole picture opened like a door showing a space within where three or four could stand. Anthony stepped inside and his friend followed him, and after showing him some clothes hanging against the wall closed the picture after them, leaving them in the dark.

"Now see what a sharp-eyed old fellow he is too," whispered his host. Anthony looked where he was guided, and perceived two pinholes through which he could see the whole length of the corridor.

"Through the centre of each eye," whispered his friend. "Is he not shrewd and secret? And now turn this way."

Anthony turned round and saw the opposite wall slowly opening; and in a moment more he stepped out and found himself in the lobby outside the little room where he had made the exercises six years ago. He heard a door close softly as he looked about him in astonishment, and on turning round saw only an innocent-looking set of shelves with a couple of books and a little pile of paper and packet of quills upon them.

"There," said Mr. Buxton, "who would suspect Tacitus his history and Juvenal his satires of guarding the passage of a Christian ecclesiastic fleeing for his life?"

Then he showed him the secret, how one shelf had to be drawn out steadily, and the nail in another pressed simultaneously, and how then the entire set of shelves swung open.

Then they went back and he showed him the spring behind the frame of the picture.

"You see the advantage of this," he went on: "on the one side you may flee upstairs, a treasonable skulking cassocked jack-priest with the lords and the commons and the Queen's Majesty barking at your heels; and on the other side you may saunter down the gallery without your beard and in a murrey doublet, a friend of Mr. Buxton's, taking the air and wondering what the devil all the clamouring be about."

Then he took him downstairs again and showed him finally the escape of which he was most proud—the entrance, designed in the cellar-staircase, to an underground passage from the cellars, which led, he told him, across to the garden-house beyond the lime-avenue.

"That is the pride of my heart," he said, "and maybe will be useful some day; though I pray not. Ah! her Grace and her honest Council are right. We Papists are a crafty and deceitful folk, Father Anthony."

The four grew very intimate during those few weeks; they had many memories and associations in common on which to build up friendship, and the aid of a common faith and a common peril with which to cement it. The gracious beauty of the house and the life at Stanfield, too, gilded it all with a very charming romance. They were all astonished at the easy intimacy with which they behaved, one to another.

Mary Corbet was obliged to return to her duties at Court at the beginning of September; and she had something of an ache at her heart as the time drew on; for she had fallen once more seriously in love with Isabel.

She said a word of it to Mr. Buxton. They were walking in the lime-avenue together after dinner on the last day of Mary's visit.

"You have a good chaplain," she said; "what an honest lad he is! and how serious and recollected! Please God he at least may escape their claws!"

"It is often so," said Mr. Buxton, "with those wholesome out-of-door boys; they grow up into such simple men of God."

"And Isabel!" said Mary, rustling round upon him as she walked. "What a great dame she is become! I used to lie on her bed and kick my heels and laugh at her; but now I would like to say my prayers to her. She is somewhat like our Lady herself, so grave and serious, and yet so warm and tender."

Mr. Buxton nodded sharply.

"I felt sure you would feel it," he said.

"Ah! but I knew her when she was just a child; so simple that I loved to startle her. But now—but now—those two ladies have done wonders with her. She has all the splendour of Mary Maxwell, and all the softness of Margaret."

"Yes," said the other meditatively; "the two ladies have done it—or, the grace of God."

Mary looked at him sideways and her lips twitched a little.

"Yes—or the grace of God, as you say."

The two laughed into each other's eyes, for they understood one another well. Presently Mary went on:

"When you and I fence together at table, she does not turn frigid like so many holy folk—or peevish and bewildered like stupid folk—but she just looks at us, and laughs far down in those deep grey eyes of hers. Oh! I love her!" ended Mary.

They walked in silence a minute or two.

"And I think I do," said Mr. Buxton softly.

"Eh?" exclaimed Mary, "you do what?" She had quite forgotten her last sentence.

"It is no matter," he said yet more softly; and would say no more.

Presently the talk fell on the Maxwells; and came round to Hubert.

"They say he would be a favourite at Court," said Mary, "had he not a wife. But her Grace likes not married men. She looked kindly upon him at Deptford, I know; and I have seen him at Greenwich. You know, of course, about Isabel?"

Mr. Buxton shook his head.

"Why, it was common talk that they would have been man and wife years ago, had not the fool apostatised."

Her companion questioned her further, and soon had the whole story out of her. "But I am thankful," ended Mary, "that it has so ended."

The next day she went back to Court; and it was with real grief that the three watched her wonderful plumed riding-hat trot along behind the top of the churchyard wall, with her woman beside her, and her little liveried troop of men following at a distance.

The days passed by, bringing strange tidings to Stanfield. News continued to reach the Catholics of the good confessions witnessed here and there in England by priests and laity. At the end of July, three priests, Garlick, Ludlam and Sympson, had been executed at Derby, and at the end of August the defeat of the Armada seemed to encourage Elizabeth yet further, and Mr. Leigh, a priest, with four laymen and Mistress Margaret Ward, died for their religion at Tyburn.

By the end of September the news of the hopeless defeat and disappearance of the Armada had by now been certified over and over again. Terrible stories had come in during August of that northward flight of all that was left of the fleet over the plunging North Sea up into the stormy coast of Scotland; then rumours began of the miseries that were falling on the Spaniards off Ireland—Catholic Ireland from which they had hoped so much. There was scarcely a bay or a cape along the west coast where some ship had not put in, with piteous entreaties for water and aid—and scarcely a bay or a cape that was not blood-guilty. Along the straight coast from Sligo Bay westwards, down the west coast, Clew Bay, Connemara, and haunted Dingle itself, where the Catholic religion under arms had been so grievously chastened eight years ago—everywhere half-drowned or half-starved Spaniards, piteously entreating, were stripped and put to the sword either by the Irish savages or the English gentlemen. The church-bells were rung in Stanfield and in every English village, and the flame of national pride and loyalty burned fiercer and higher than ever.

On the last day of September Isabel, just before dinner in her room, heard the trot of a couple of horses coming up the short drive, and on going downstairs almost ran against Hubert as he came from the corridor into the hall, as the servant ushered him in.

The two stopped and looked at one another in silence.

Hubert was flushed with hard riding and looked excited; Isabel's face showed nothing but pleasure and surprise. The servant too stopped, hesitating.

Then Isabel put out her hand, smiling; and her voice was natural and controlled.

"Why, Mr. Hubert," she said, "it is you! Come through this way"; and she nodded to the servant, who went forward and opened the door of the little parlour and stood back, as Isabel swept by him.

When the door was closed, and the servant's footsteps had died away, Hubert, as he stood facing Isabel, spoke at last.

"Mistress Isabel," he said almost imploringly, "what can I say to you? Your home has been wrecked; and partly through those wild and foolish words of mine; and you repay it by that act of kindness to my wife! I am come to ask your pardon, and to thank you. I only reached home last night."

"Ah! that was nothing," said Isabel gently; "and as for the house——"

"As for the house," he said, "I was not master of myself when I said those words that Grace told you of; and I entreat you to let me repair the damage."

"No, no," she said, "Anthony has given orders; that will all be done."

"But what can I do then?" he cried passionately; "if you but knew my sorrow—and—and—more than that, my——"

Isabel had raised her grave eyes and was looking him full in the face now; and he stopped abashed.

"How is Grace, and Mercy?" she asked in perfectly even tones.

"Oh! Isabel——" he began; and again she looked at him, and then went to the door.

"I hear Mr. Buxton," she said; and steps came along through the hall; she opened the door as he came up. Mr. Buxton stopped abruptly, and the two men drew themselves up and seemed to stiffen, ever so slightly. A shade of aggressive contempt came on Hubert's keen brown face that towered up so near the low oak ceiling; while Mr. Buxton's eyelids just drooped, and his features seemed to sharpen. There was an unpleasant silence: Isabel broke it.

"You remember Master Hubert Maxwell?" she said almost entreatingly. He smiled kindly at her, but his face hardened again as he turned once more to Hubert.

"I remember the gentleman perfectly," he said, "and he no doubt knows me, and why I cannot ask him to remain and dine with us."

Hubert smiled brutally.

"It is the old story of course, the Faith! I must ask your pardon, sir, for intruding. The difficulty never came into my mind. The truth is that I have lived so long now among Protestants that I had quite forgotten what Catholic charity is like!"

He said this with such extreme bitterness and fury that Isabel put out her hand instinctively to Mr. Buxton, who smiled at her once more, and pressed it in his own. Hubert laughed again sharply; his face grew white under the tan, and his lips wrinkled back once or twice.

"So, if you can spare me room to pass," he went on in the same tone, "I will begone to the inn."

Mr. Buxton stepped aside from the door, and Hubert bowed to Isabel so low that it was almost an insult in itself, and strode out, his spurs ringing on the oak boards.

When he half turned outside the front door to beckon to his groom to bring up the horses, he became aware that Isabel was beside him.

"Hubert," she said, "Hubert, I cannot bear this."

There were tears in her voice, and he could not help turning and looking at her. Her face, more grave and transparent than ever, was raised to his; her red down-turned lips were trembling, and her eyes were full of a great emotion. He turned away again sharply.

"Hubert," she said again, "I was not born a Catholic, and I do not feel like Mr. Buxton. And—and I do thank you for coming; and for your desire to repair the house; and—and will you give my love to Grace?"

Then he suddenly turned to her with such passion in his eyes that she shrank back. At the same moment the groom brought up the horses; he turned and mounted without a word, but his eyes were dim with love and anger and jealousy. Then he drove his spurs into his great grey mare, and Isabel watched him dash between the iron gates, with his groom only half mounted holding back his own plunging horse. Then she went within doors again.

CHAPTER V
JOSEPH LACKINGTON

It was a bitter ride back to Great Keynes for Hubert. He had just returned from watching the fifty vessels, which were all that were left of the Great Armada, pass the Blaskets, still under the nominal command of Medina Sidonia, on their miserable return to Spain; and he had come back as fast as sails could carry him, round the stormy Land's-End up along the south coast to Rye, where on his arrival he had been almost worshipped by the rejoicing townsfolk. Yet all through his voyage and adventures, at any rate since his interview with her at Rye, it had been the face of Isabel there, and not of Grace, that had glimmered to him in the dark, and led him from peril to peril. Then, at last, on his arrival at home, he had heard of the disaster to the Dower House, and his own unintended share in it; and of Isabel's generous visit to his wife; and at that he had ordered his horse abruptly over-night and ridden off without a word of explanation to Grace on the following morning. And he had been met by a sneering man who would not sit at table with him, and who was the protector and friend of Isabel.

He rode up through the village just after dark and in through the gatehouse up to the steps. A man ran to open the door, and as Hubert came through told him that a stranger had ridden down from London and had arrived at mid-day, and that he had been waiting ever since.

"I gave the gentleman dinner in the cloister parlour, sir; and he is at supper now," added the man.

Hubert nodded and pushed through the hall. He heard his name called timidly from upstairs, and looking up saw his wife's golden head over the banisters.

"Well!" he said.

"Ah, it is you. I am so glad."

"Who else should it be?" said Hubert, and passed through towards the cloister wing, and opened the door of the little parlour where Isabel and Mistress Margaret had sat together years before, the night of Mr. James' return, and of the girl's decision.

A stranger rose up hastily as he came in, and bowed with great deference. Hubert knew his face, but could not remember his name.

"I ask your pardon, Mr. Maxwell; but your man would take no denial," and he indicated the supper-table with a steaming dish and a glass jug of wine ruddy in the candlelight. Hubert looked at him curiously.

"I know you, sir," he said, "but I cannot put a name to your face."

"Lackington," said the man with a half smile; "Joseph Lackington."

Hubert still stared; and then suddenly burst into a short laugh.

"Why, yes," he said; "I know now. My father's servant."

The man bowed.

"Formerly, sir; and now agent to Sir Francis Walsingham," he said, with something of dignity in his manner.

Hubert saw the hint, but could not resist a small sneer.

"Why, I am pleased to see you," he said. "You have come to see your old—home?" and he threw himself into a chair and stretched his legs to the blaze, for he was stiff with riding. Lackington instantly sat down too, for his pride was touched.

"It was not for that, Mr. Maxwell," he said almost in the tone of an equal, "but on a mission for Sir Francis."

Hubert looked at him a moment as he sat there in the candlelight, with his arm resting easily on the table. He was plainly prosperous, and was even dressed with some distinction; his reddish beard was trimmed to a point; his high forehead was respectably white and bald; and his seals hung from his belt beside his dagger with an air of ease and solidity. Perhaps he was of some importance; at any rate, Sir Francis Walsingham was. Hubert sat up a little.

"A mission to me?" he said.

Lackington nodded.

"A few questions on a matter of state."

He drew from his pouch a paper signed by Sir Francis authorising him as an agent, for one month, and dated three days back; and handed it to Hubert.

"I obtained that from Sir Francis on Monday, as you will see. You can trust me implicitly."

"Will the business take long?" asked Hubert, handing the paper back.

"No, Mr. Maxwell; and I must be gone in an hour in any case. I have to be at Rye at noon to-morrow; and I must sleep at Mayfield to-night."

"At Rye," said Hubert, "why I came from there yesterday."

Lackington bowed again, as if he were quite aware of this; but said nothing.

"Then I will sup here," went on Hubert, "and we will talk meantime."

When a place had been laid for him, he drew his chair round to the table and began to eat.

"May I begin at once?" asked Lackington, who had finished.

Hubert nodded.

"Then first I believe it to be a fact that you spoke with Mistress Isabel Norris on board the *Elizabeth* at Rye on the tenth of August last."

Hubert had started violently at her name; but did his utmost to gain outward command of himself again immediately.

"Well?" he said.

—"And with Master Anthony Norris, lately made a priest beyond the seas."

"That is a lie," said Hubert.

Lackington politely lifted his eyebrows.

"Indeed?" he said. "That he was made a priest, or that you spoke with him?"

"That I know aught of him," said Hubert. His heart was beating furiously.

Lackington made a note rather ostentatiously; he could see that Hubert was frightened, and thought that it was because of a possible accusation of having dealings with a traitor.

"And as regards Mistress Norris," he said judicially, with his pencil raised, "you deny having spoken with her?"

Hubert was thinking furiously. Then he saw that Lackington knew too much for its being worth his own while to deny it.

"No, I never denied that," he said, lifting his fork to his mouth; and he went on eating with a deliberate ease as Lackington again made a note.

The next question was a home-thrust.

"Where are they both now?" asked Lackington, looking at him. Hubert's mind laboured like a mill.

"I do not know," he said.

"You swear it?"

"I swear it."

"Then Mistress Norris has changed her plans?" said Lackington swiftly.

"What do you mean by that?"

"Why she told you where they were going when you met?" said the other in a remonstrating tone.

Hubert suddenly saw the game. If the authorities really knew that, it would have been a useless question. He stared at Lackington with an admirable vacancy.

"Indeed she did not," he said. "For aught I know, they—she is in France again."

"They?" said Lackington shrewdly. "Then you do know somewhat of the priest?"

But Hubert was again too sharp.

"Only what you told me just now, when you said he was at Rye. I supposed you were telling the truth."

Lackington passed his hand smoothly over his mouth and beard, and smiled. Either Hubert was very sharp or else he had told everything; and he did not believe him sharp.

"Thank you, Mr. Maxwell," he said, with a complete dropping of his judicial manner. "I will not pretend not to be disappointed; but I believe what you say about France is true; and that it is no use looking for him further."

Hubert experienced an extraordinary relief. He had saved Isabel. He drank off a glass of claret. "Tell me everything," he said.

"Well," said Lackington, "Mr. Thomas Hamon is my informant. He sent up to Sir Francis the message that a lady of the name of Norris had been introduced to him at Rye; because he thought he remembered some stir in the county several years ago about some reconciliations to Rome connected with that name. Of course we knew everything about that: and we have our agents at the seminaries too; so we concluded that she was one of our birds; the rest, of course, was guesswork. Mr. Norris has certainly left Douai for England; and he may possibly even now be in England; but from your information and others', I now believe that Mistress Isabel came across first, and that she found the country too hot, what with the Spaniards and all; and that she returned to France at once. Of course during that dreadful week, Mr. Maxwell, we could not be certain of all vessels that came and went; so I think she just slipped across again; and that they are both waiting in France. We shall keep good watch now at the ports, I can promise you."

Hubert's emotions were varied during this speech. First shame at having entirely forgotten the mayor of Rye and his own introduction of Isabel to him; then astonishment at the methods of Walsingham's agents; and lastly intense triumph and relief at having put them off Isabel's track. For Anthony, too, he had nothing but kindly feelings; so, on the whole, he thought he had done well for his friends.

The two talked a little longer; Lackington was a stimulating companion from both his personality and his position; and Hubert found himself almost sorry when his companion said he must be riding on to Mayfield. As he walked out with him to the front door, he suddenly thought of Mr. Buxton again and his reception in the afternoon. They had wandered in their conversation so far from the Norrises by now that he felt sure he could speak of him without doing them any harm. So, as they stood on the steps together, waiting for Lackington's horse to come round, he suddenly said:

"Do you know aught of one Buxton, who lives somewhere near Tonbridge, I think?"

"Buxton, Buxton?" said the other.

"I met him in town once," went on Hubert smoothly; "a little man, dark, with large eyes, and looks somewhat like a Frenchman."

"Buxton, Buxton?" said the other again. "A Papist, is he not?"

"Yes," said Hubert, hoping to get some information against him.

"A friend?" asked Lackington.

"No," said Hubert with such vehemence that Lackington looked at him.

"I remember him," he said in a moment; "he was imprisoned at Wisbeach six or seven years ago. But I do not think he has been in trouble since. You wish, you wish——?" he went on interrogatively.

"Nothing," said Hubert; but Lackington saw the hatred in his eyes.

The horses came round at this moment; and Lackington said good-bye to Hubert with a touch of the old deference again, and mounted. Hubert watched him out under the gatehouse-lamp into the night beyond, and then he went in again, pondering.

His wife was waiting for him in the hall now—a delicate golden-haired figure, with pathetic blue eyes turned up to him. She ran to him and took his arm timidly in her two hands.

"Oh! I am glad that man has gone, Hubert."

He looked down at her almost contemptuously.

"Why, you know nothing of him!" he said.

"Not much," she said, "but he asked me so many questions."

Hubert started and looked suddenly at her, in terror.

"Oh, Hubert!" she said, shrinking back frightened.

"Questions!" he said, seizing her hands. "Questions of whom?"

"Of—of—Mistress Isabel Norris," she said, almost crying.

"And—and—what did you say? Did you tell him?"

"Oh, Hubert!—I am so sorry—ah! do not look like that."

"What did you say? What did you say?" he said between his teeth.

"I—I—told a lie, Hubert; I said I had never seen her."

Hubert took his wife suddenly in his two arms and kissed her three or four times.

"You darling, you darling!" he said; and then stooped and picked her up, and carried her upstairs, with her head against his cheek, and her tears running down because he was pleased with her, instead of angry.

They went upstairs and he set her down softly outside the nursery door.

"Hush," she said, smiling up at him; and then softly opened the door and listened, her finger on her lip; there was no sound from within; then she pushed the door open gently, and the wife and husband went in.

There was a shaded taper still burning in a high bracket where an image of the Mother of God had stood in the Catholic days of the house. Hubert glanced up at it and remembered it, with just a touch at his heart. Beneath it was a little oak cot, where his four-year-old boy lay sleeping; the mother went across and bent over it, and Hubert leaned his brown sinewy hands on the end of the cot and watched him. There his son lay, with tangled curls on the pillow; his finger was on his lips as if he bade silence even to thought. Hubert looked up, and just above the bed, where the crucifix used to hang when he himself had slept in this nursery, probably on the very same nail, he thought to himself, was a rusty Spanish spur that he himself had found in a sea-chest of the *San Juan*. The boy had hung up with a tarry bit of string this emblem of his father's victory, as a protection while he slept.

The child stirred in his sleep and murmured as the two watched him.

"Father's home again," whispered the mother. "It is all well. Go to sleep again."

When she looked up again to her husband, he was gone.

It was not often that Hubert had regrets for the Faith he had lost; but to-night things had conspired to prick him. There was his rebuff from Mr. Buxton; there was the sight of Isabel in the dignified grace that he had noticed so plainly before; there had been the interview with the ex-Catholic servant, now a spy of the Government, and a remorseless enemy of all Catholics; and lastly there were the two little external reminders of the niche and the nail over his son's bed.

He sat long before the fire in Sir Nicholas' old room, now his own study. As he lay back and looked about him, how different this all was, too! The mantelpiece was almost unaltered; the Maxwell devices, two-headed eagles, hurcheons and saltires, on crowded shields, interlaced with the motto *Reviresco*, all newly gilded since his own accession to the estate, rose up in deep shadow and relief; but over it, instead of the little old picture of the Vernacle that he remembered as a child, hung his own sword. Was that a sign of progress? he wondered. The tapestry on the east wall was the same, a hawking scene with herons and ladies in immense headdresses that he had marvelled at as a boy. But then the books on the shelves to the right of the door, they were different; there had been old devotional books in his father's time, mingled strangely with small works on country life and sports; now the latter only remained, and the nearest to a devotional book was a volume of a mystical herbalist who identified plants with virtues, strangely and ingeniously. Then the prie-dieu, where the beads had hung and the little wooden shield with the Five Wounds painted upon it—that was gone; and in its place hung a cupboard where he kept a crossbow and a few tools for it; and old hawk-lures and jesses and the like.

Then he lay back again, and thought.

Had he then behaved unworthily? This old Faith that had been handed down from father and son for generations; that had been handed to him too as the most precious heirloom of all—for which his father had so gladly suffered fines and imprisonment, and risked death—he had thrown it over, and for what? For Isabel, he confessed to himself; and then the—the Power that stands behind the visible had cheated him and withdrawn that for which he had paid over that great price. Was that a reckless and brutal bargain on his side—to throw over this strange delicate thing called the Faith for which so many millions had lived and died, all for a woman's love? A curious kind of family pride in the Faith began to prick him. After all, was not honour in a manner bound up with it too; and most of all when such heavy penalties attached themselves to the profession of it? Was that the moment when he should be the first of his line to abandon it?

Reviresco—"I renew my springtide." But was not this a strange grafting—a spur for a crucifix, a crossbow for a place of prayer? *Reviresco*— There was sap indeed in the old tree; but from what soil did it draw its strength?

His heart began to burn with something like shame, as it had burned now and again at intervals during these past years. Here he lay back in his father's chair, in his father's room, the first Protestant of the Maxwells. Then he passed on to a memory.

As he closed his eyes, he could see even now the chapel upstairs, with the tapers alight and the stiff figure of the priest in the midst of the glow; he could smell the flowers on the altar, the June roses strewn on the floor in the old manner, and their fresh dewy scent mingled with the fragrance of the rich incense in an intoxicating chord; he could hear the rustle that emphasised the silence, as his mother rose from his side and went up for communion, and the breathing of the servants behind him.

Then for contrast he remembered the whitewashed church where he attended now with his wife, Sunday by Sunday, the pulpit occupied by the black figure of the virtuous Mr. Bodder pronouncing his discourse, the great texts that stood out in their new paint from the walls, the table that stood out unashamed and sideways in the midst of the chancel. And which of the two worships was most like God?...

Then he compared the worshippers in either mode. Well, Drake, his hero, was a convinced Protestant; the bravest man he had ever met or dreamed of—fiery, pertinacious, gloriously insolent. He thought of his sailors, on whom a portion of Drake's spirit fell, their gallantry, their fearlessness of death and of all that comes after; of Mr. Bodder, who was now growing middle-aged in the Vicarage—yes, indeed, they were all admirable in various ways, but were they like Christ?

On the other hand, his father, in spite of his quick temper, his mother, brother, aunt, the priests who came and went by night, Isabel—and at that he stopped: and like a deep voice in his ear rose up the last tremendous question, What if the Catholic Religion be true after all? And at that the supernatural began to assert itself. It seemed as if the empty air were full of this question, rising in intensity and emphasis. What if it is true? What if it is true? *What if it is true?*

He sat bolt upright and looked sharply round the room; the candles burned steadily in the sconce near the door. The tapestry lifted and dropped noiselessly in the draught; the dark corners beyond the press and in the window recesses suggested presences that waited; the wide chimney sighed suddenly once.

Was that a voice in his ear just now, or only in his heart? But in either case— —

He made an effort to command himself, and looked again steadily round the room; but there seemed no one there. But what if the old tale be true? In that case he is not alone in this little oak room, for there is no such thing as loneliness. In that case he is sitting in full sight of Almighty God, whom he has insulted; and of the saints whose power he has repudiated; and of the angels good and bad who have— — Ah! what was that? There had seemed to come a long sigh somewhere behind him; on his left surely.—What was it? Some wandering soul? Was it, could it be the soul of one who had loved him and desired to warn him before it was too late? Could it have been— — and then it came again; and the hair prickled on his head.

How deathly still it is, and how cold! Ah! was that a rustle outside; a tap?... In God's name, who can that be?...

And then Hubert licked his dry lips and brought them together and smiled at Grace, who had come down, opening the doors as she came, to see why he had not come to bed.

Bah! what a superstitious fool he was, after all!

CHAPTER VI
A DEPARTURE

The months went by happily at Stanfield; and, however ill went the fortunes of the Church elsewhere, here at least were peace and prosperity. Most discouraging news indeed did reach them from time to time. The severe penalties now enacted against the practice of the Catholic Religion were being enforced with great vigour, and the weak members of the body began to fail. Two priests had apostatised at Chichester earlier in the year, one of them actually at the scaffold on Broyle Heath; and then in December there were two more recantations at Paul's Cross. Those Catholics too who threw up the Faith generally became the most aggressive among the persecutors, to testify to their own consciences, as well to the Protestants, of the sincerity of their conversion.

But in Stanfield the Church flourished, and Anthony had the great happiness of receiving his first convert in the person of Mr. Rowe, the young owner of a house called East Maskells, separated from Stanfield Place by a field-path of under a mile in length, though the road round was over two; and the comings and goings were frequent now between the two houses. Mr. Rowe was at present unmarried, and had his aunt to keep house for him, a tolerant old maiden lady who had conformed placidly to the Reformed Religion thirty years before, and was now grown content with it. Several "schismatics" too—as those Catholics were called who attended their parish church—had waxed bolder, and given up their conformity to the Establishment; so it was a happy and courageous flock that gathered Sunday by Sunday at Stanfield Place.

Just before Christmas, Anthony received a long and affectionate letter from James Maxwell, who was still at Douai.

"The Rector will still have me here," he wrote, "and shows me to the young men as if I were a kind of warrior; which is bad for pride; but then he humbles me again by telling me I am of more use here as an example, than I should be in England; and that humbles me again. So I am content to stay. It is a humbling thing, too, to find young men who can tell me the history of my arms and legs better than I know it myself. But the truth is, I can never walk well again—yet *laudetur Jesus Christus*."

Then James Maxwell wrote a little about his grief for Hubert; gave a little news of foreign movements among the Catholics; and finally ended as follows:

"At last I understand who your friend was behind Bow Church, who stuttered and played the Catholic so well. It was our old servant Lackington; who turned Protestant and entered Walsingham's service. I hear all this from one P. lately in the same affairs, but now turned to Christ his service instead; and who has entered here as a student. So beware of him; he has a pointed beard now, and a bald forehead. I hear, too, from the same source that he was on your track when you landed, but now thinks you to be in France. However, he knows of you; so I counsel you not to abide over long in one place. Perhaps you may go to Lancashire; that is like heaven itself for Catholics. Their zeal and piety there are beyond praise; but I hear they somewhat lack priests. God keep you always, my dear Brother; and may the Queen of Heaven intercede for you. Pray for me."

Soon after the New Year, Mary Corbet was able to get away from Court and come down again to her friends for a month or two at Stanfield.

During her stay they all had an adventure together at East Maskells. They had been out a long expedition into the woods one clear frosty day and rode in just at sunset for an early supper with Mr. Rowe and his aunt.

They had left their horses at the stable and come in round the back of the house; so that they missed the servant Miss Rowe had placed at the front door to warn them, and came straight into the winter-parlour, where they found Miss Rowe in conversation with an ecclesiastic. There was no time to retreat; and Anthony in a moment more found himself being introduced to a minister he had met at Lambeth more than once—the Reverend Robert Carr, who had held the odd title of "Archbishop's Curate" and the position of minister in charge of the once collegiate church of All Saints', Maidstone, ever since the year '59. He had ridden up from Maidstone for supper and lodging, and was on his way to town.

Anthony managed to interrupt Miss Rowe before she came to his assumed name Capell, and remarked rather loudly that he had met Mr. Carr before; who recognised him too, and greeted him by his real name.

It was an uncomfortable situation, as Mr. Carr was quite unaware of the religion of five out of six of those present, and very soon began to give voice to his views on Papistry. He was an oldish man by now, and of some importance in Maidstone, where he had been appointed Jurat by the Corporation, and was a very popular and influential man.

"The voice of the people," he said in the midst of a conversation on the national feeling towards Spain, "that is what we must hearken to. Even sovereigns themselves must come to that some day. They must rule by obeying; as man does with God's laws in nature."

"Would you say that, sir, of her Grace?" asked Mary Corbet meekly.

"I should, madam; though I fear she has injured her power by her behaviour this year. It was her people who saved her.—Hawkins, who is now ruined as he says; my lord Howard, who has paid from his own purse for the meat and drink of her Grace's soldiers, and those who fought with them; and not her Grace, who saved them; or Leicester, now gone to his account, who sat at Tilbury and did the bowing and the prancing and the talking while Hawkins and the rest did the fighting. No, madam, it is the voice of the people to which we must hearken."

This was rather confused and dangerous talking too; but here was plainly a man to be humoured; he looked round him with a suffused face and the eye of a cock, and a little white plume on his forehead increased his appearance of pugnacity.

"It is the same in religion," he said, when all preserved a deferential silence; "it is that that lies at the root of papist errors. As you know very well," he went on, turning suddenly on Anthony, "our bishops do nothing to guide men's minds; they only seem to: they ride atop like the figure on a cock-horse, but it is the legs beneath that do the work and the guiding too: now that is right and good; and the Church of England will prosper so long as she goes like that. But if the bishops try to rule they will find their mistake. Now the Popish Church is not like that; she holds that power comes from above, that the Pope guides the bishops, the bishops the priests, and the priests the people."

"And the Holy Ghost the Pope; is it not so, sir?" asked Mr. Buxton.

Mr. Carr turned an eye on him.

"So they hold, sir," he said after a pause.

"They think then, sir, that the shepherds guide the sheep?" asked Anthony humbly.

Mary Corbet gave a yelp of laughter; but when Mr. Carr looked at her she was grave and deferential again. Miss Rowe looked entreatingly from face to face. The minister did not notice Anthony's remark; but swept on again on what was plainly his favourite theme,—the infallibility of the people. It was a doctrine that was hardly held yet by any; but the next century was to see its gradual rise until it reached its climax in the Puritanism of the Stuart times. It was true, as Mr. Carr said, that Elizabeth had ruled by obeying; and that the people of England, encouraged by success in resisting foreign domination, were about to pass on to the second position of resisting any domination at all.

Presently he pulled out of his pocket a small printed sheet, and was soon declaiming from it. It was not very much to the point, except as illustrating the national spirit which he believed so divine. It was a ballad describing the tortures which the Spaniards had intended to inflict upon the heretic English, and began:

> "All you that list to look and see
> What profit comes from Spain,
> And what the Pope and Spaniards both
> Prepared for our gain.
> Then turn your eyes and lend your ears
> And you shall hear and see
> What courteous minds, what gentle hearts,
> They bear to thee and me!

And it ended in the same spirit:

> "Be these the men that are so mild
> Whom some so holy call!
> The Lord defend our noble Queen
> And country from them all!"

"There!" the minister cried when he had done, "that is what the Papists are like! Trust me; I know them. I should know one in a moment if he ventured into this room, by his crafty face. But the Lord will defend His own Englishmen; nay! He has done so. 'God blew and they were scattered,'" he ended, quoting from the Armada medal.

As the four rode home by pairs across the field-path in the frosty moonlight Mr. Buxton lamented to Anthony the effect of the Armada.

"The national spirit is higher than ever," he said, "and it will be the death of Catholicism here for the present. Our country squires, I fear, faithful Catholics to this time, are beginning to wonder and question. When will our Catholic kings learn that Christ His Kingdom is not of this world? Philip has smitten the Faith in England with the weapon which he drew in its defence, as he thought."

"I was once of that national spirit myself," said Anthony.

"I remember you were," said Mr. Buxton, smiling; "and what grace has done to you it may do to others."

The spring went by, and in the week after Easter, James' news about Lancashire was verified by a letter from a friend of Mr. Buxton's, a Mr. Norreys, the owner of one of the staunch Catholic houses, Speke Hall, on the bank of the Mersey.

"Here," he wrote, "by the mercy of God there is no lack of priests, though there be none to spare; my own chaplain says mass by dispensation thrice on Sunday; but on the moors the sheep look up and are not fed; and such patient sheep! I heard but last week of a church where the folk resort, priest or no, each Sunday to the number of two hundred, and are led by a lector in devotion, ending with an act of spiritual communion made all together. These damnable heresies of which the apostle wrote have not poisoned the springs of sound doctrine; some of us here know naught yet of Elizabeth and her supremacy, or even of seven-wived Harry his reformation. Send us then, dear friend, a priest, or at least the promise of one; lest we perish quite."

Mr. Buxton had a sore struggle with himself over this letter; but at last he carried it to Anthony.

"Read that," he said; and stood waiting.

Anthony looked up when he had done.

"I am your chaplain," he said, "but I am God's priest first."

"Yes, dear lad," said his friend, "I feared you would say so; and I will say so to Norreys"; and he left the room at once.

And so at last it came to be arranged that Anthony should leave for Lancashire at the end of July; and that after his departure Stanfield should be served occasionally by the priest who lived on the outskirts of Tonbridge; but the daily mass would have to cease, and that was a sore trouble to Mr. Buxton. No definite decision could be made as to when Anthony could return; that must wait until he saw the needs of Lancashire; but he hoped to be able at least to pay a visit to Stanfield again in the spring of the following year.

It was arranged also, of course, that Isabel should accompany her brother. They were both of large independent means, and could travel in some dignity; and her presence would be under these circumstances a protection as well as a comfort to Anthony. It would need very great sharpness to detect the seminary priest under Anthony's disguise, and amid the surroundings of his cavalcade of four or five armed servants, a French maid, and a distinguished-looking lady.

Yet, in spite of this, Mr. Buxton resolved to do his utmost to prevent Isabel from going to Lancashire; partly, of course, he disliked the thought of the dangers and hardships that she was certain to encounter; but the real motive was that he had fallen very deeply in love with her. It was her exceptional serenity that seemed to him her greatest charm; her movements, her face, her grey eyes, the very folds of her dress seemed to breathe with it; and to one of Mr. Buxton's temperament such a presence was cool and sweet and strangely fascinating.

It was now April, and he resolved to devote the next month or two to preparing her for his proposal; and he wrote frankly to Mary Corbet telling her how matters stood, entreating her to come down for July and counsel him. Mary wrote back at once, rather briefly, promising to come; but not encouraging him greatly.

"I would I could cheer you more," she wrote; "of course I have not seen Isabel since January; but, unless she has changed, I do not think she will marry you. I am writing plainly you see, as you ask in your letter. But I can still say, God prosper you."

As the spring went by and the summer came on, Isabel grew yet more silent. As the evenings began to lengthen out she used to spend much time before and after supper in walking up and down the clipped lime avenue between the east end of the church and the great gates that looked over the meadows across which the stream and the field-path ran towards East Maskells. Mr. Buxton would watch her sometimes from an upstairs window, himself unseen, and occasionally would go out and talk with her; but he found it harder than he used to get on to intimate relations; and he began to suspect that he had displeased her in some way, and that Mary Corbet was right. In the afternoon she and Anthony would generally ride out together, once or twice going round by Penshurst, and their host would torture himself by his own indecision as regards accompanying them; sometimes doing so, sometimes refraining, and regretting whichever he did. More and more he began to look forward to Mary's coming and the benefit of her advice; and at last, at the end of June, she came.

Their first evening together was delightful for them all. She was happy at her escape from Court; her host was happy at the prospect of her counsel; and all four were happy at being together again.

They did not meet till supper, and even that was put off an hour, because Mary had not come, and when she did arrive she was full of excitement.

"I will tell you all at supper," she said to her host, whom she met in the hall. "Oh! how late I am!" and she whirled past him and upstairs without another word.

"I will first give you the news in brief," she said, when Anthony had said grace and they were seated, all four of them as before; and the trumpet-flourish was silent that had announced the approach of the venison.

"Mutton's new chaplain, Dr. Bancroft, will be in trouble soon; he hath been saying favourable things for some of us poor papists, and hath rated the Precisians soundly. Sir Francis Knollys is wroth with him; but that is no matter.—Her Grace played at cards till two of the clock this morning, and that is why I am so desperate sleepy to-night, for I had to sit up too; and that is a great matter.—Drake and Norris, 'tis said, have whipped the dons again at Corunna; and the Queen has sworn to pull my lord Essex his ears for going with them and adventuring his precious self; and that is no matter at all, but will do him good.—George Luttrell hath put up a coat of arms in his hall at Dunster, which is a great matter to him, but to none else;—and I have robbed a highwayman this day in the beech woods this side of Groombridge."

"Dear lady," said Mr. Buxton resignedly, as the others looked up startled, "you are too swift for our dull rustic ears; we will begin at the end, if you please. Is it true you have robbed an highwayman?"

"It is perfectly true," she said, and unlatched a ruby brooch, made heart-shape, from her dress. "There is the plunder," and she held it out for inspection.

"Then tell us the tale," said Anthony.

"It would be five of the clock," said Mary, "as we came through Groombridge, and then into the woods beyond. I had bidden my knaves ride on before with my woman; I came down into a dingle where there was a stream; and, to tell the truth, I had my head down and was a-nodding, when my horse stopped; and I looked up of a sudden and there was a man on a bay mare, with a mask to his mouth, a gay green suit, a brown beard turning grey, and this ruby brooch at his throat; and he had caught my bridle. I saw him start when I lifted my head, as if he were taken aback. I said nothing, but he led my horse off the road down among the trees with a deep little thicket where none could see us. As we went I was thinking like a windmill; for I knew I had seen the little red brooch before.

"When we reached the little open space, I asked him what he wished with me.

"'Your purse, madam,' said he.

"'My woman hath it,' said I.

"'Your jewels then, madam,' said he.

"'My woman hath them,' said I, 'save this paste buckle in my hat, to which you are welcome.' It was diamonds, you know; but I knew he would not know that.

"'What a mistake,' I said, 'to stop the mistress and let the maid go free!'

"'Nay,' he said, 'I am glad of it; for at least I will have a dance with the mistress; and I could not with the maid.'

"'You are welcome to that,' I said, and I slipped off my horse, to humour him, and even as I slipped off I knew who he was, for although many have red brooches, and many brown beards turning grey, few have both together; but I said nothing. And there—will you believe it?—we danced under the beech-trees like Phyllis and Corydon, or whoever they are that Sidney is always prating of; or like two fools, I would sooner say. Then when we had done, I made him a curtsey.

"'Now you must help me up,' said I, and he mounted me without a word, for he was a stoutish gallant and somewhat out of breath. And then what did the fool do but try to kiss me, and as he lifted his arm I snatched the brooch and put spur to my horse, and as we went up the bank I screamed at him, 'Claude, you fool, go home to your wife and take shame to yourself.' And when I was near the road I looked back, and he still stood there all agape."

"And what was his name?" asked Anthony.

"Nay, nay, I have mocked him enough. And I know four Claudes, so you need not try to guess."

When supper was over, Mr. Buxton and Mary walked up and down the south path of the garden between the yews, while the other two sat just outside the hall window on a seat placed on the tiled terrace that ran round the house.

"How I have longed for you to come, Mistress Mary," he said, "and counsel me of the matter we wrote about. Tell me what to do."

Mary looked meditatively out to the strip of moon that was rising out to the east in the June sky. Then she looked tenderly at her friend.

"I hate to pain you," she said, "but cannot you see that it is impossible? I may be wrong; but I think her heart is so given to our Saviour that there is no love of that sort left."

"Ah, how can you say that?" he cried; "the love of the Saviour does not hinder earthly love; it purifies and transfigures it."

"Yes," said Mary gravely, "it is often so—but the love of the true spouse of Christ is different. That leaves no room for an earthly bridegroom."

Mr. Buxton was silent a moment or two.

"You mean it is the love of the consecrated soul?"

Mary bowed her head. "But I cannot be sure," she added.

"Then what shall I do?" he said again, almost piteously; and Mary could see even in the faint moonlight that his pleasant face was all broken up and quivering. She laid her hand gently on his arm, and her rings flashed.

"You must be very patient," she said, "very full of deference—and grave. You must not be ardent nor impetuous, but speak slowly and reverently to her, but at no great length; be plain with her; do not look in her face, and do not show anxiety or despair or hope. You need not fear that your love will not be plain to her. Indeed, I think she knows it already."

"Why, I have not——" he began.

"I know you have not spoken to her; but I saw that she only looked at you once during supper, and that was when your face was turned from her; she does not wish to look you in the eyes."

"Ah, she hates me," he sighed.

"Do not be foolish," said Mary, "she honours you, and loves you, and is grieved for your grief; but I do not think she will marry you."

"And when shall I speak?" he asked.

"You must wait; God will make the opportunity—in any case. You must not attempt to make it. That would terrify her."

"And you will speak for me."

Mary smiled at him.

"Dear friend," she said, "sometimes I think you do not know us at all. Do you not see that Isabel is greater than all that? What she knows, she knows. I could tell her nothing."

The days passed on; the days of the last month of the Norrises' stay at Stanfield. Half-way through the month came the news of the Oxford executions.

"Ah! listen to this," cried Mr. Buxton, coming out to them one evening in the garden with a letter in his hand. "'Humphrey Prichard,'" he read, "'made a good end. He protested he was condemned for the Catholic Faith;

that he willingly died for it; that he was a Catholic. One of their ministers laughed at him, saying he was a poor ignorant fellow who knew not what it was to be a Catholic. 'I know very well;' said Humphrey, 'though I cannot say it in proper divinity language.' There is the Religion for you!" went on Mr. Buxton; "all meet there, wise and simple alike. There is no difference; no scholarship is needed for faith. 'I know what it is,' cried Humphrey, 'though I cannot explain it!'"

The news came to Anthony just when he needed it; he felt he had done so little to teach his flock now he was to leave them; but if he had only done something to keep alive the fire of faith, he had not lost his time; and so he went about his spiritual affairs with new heart, encouraging the wavering, whom he was to leave, warning the over-confident, urging the hesitating, and saying good-bye to them all. Isabel went with him sometimes; or sometimes walked or rode with Mary, and was silent for the most part in public. The master of the house himself did his affairs, and carried a heavier heart each day. And at last the opportunity came which Mary had predicted.

He had come in one evening after a hot ride alone over to Tonbridge on some business with the priest there; and had dressed for supper immediately on coming in.

As there was still nearly an hour before supper, he went out to walk up and down the same yew-alley near the garden-house where he had walked with Mary. Anthony and Isabel had returned a little later from East Maskells, and they too had dressed early. Isabel threw a lace shawl over her head, and betook herself too to the alley; and there she turned a corner and almost ran into her host.

It was, as Mary had said, a God-made opportunity. Neither time nor place could have been improved. If externals were of any value to this courtship, all that could have helped was there. The setting of the picture was perfect; a tall yew-hedge ran down the northern side of the walk, cut, as Bacon recommended, not fantastically but "with some pretty pyramids"; a strip of turf separated it from the walk, giving a sense both of privacy and space; on the south side ran flower-beds in the turf, with yews and cypresses planted here and there, and an oak paling beyond; to the east lay the "fair mount," again recommended by the same authority, but not so high, and with but one ascent; to the west the path darkened under trees, and over all rose up against the sunset sky the tall grotesque towers and vanes of the garden-house. The flowers burned with that ember-like glow which may be seen on summer evenings, and poured out their scent; the air was sweet and cool, and white moths were beginning to poise and stir among the blossoms. The two actors on this scene too were not unworthy of it; his dark velvet and lace with the glimmer of diamonds here and there, and his delicate bearded clean-cut face, a little tanned, thrown into relief by the spotless crisp ruff beneath, and above all his air of strength and refinement and self-possession—all combined to make him a formidable stormer of a girl's heart. And as he looked on her—on her clear almost luminous face and great eyes, shrined in the drooping lace shawl, through which a jewel or two in her black hair glimmered, her upright slender figure in its dark sheath, and the hand, white and cool, that held her shawl together over her breast—he had a pang of hope and despair at once, at the sudden sense of need of this splendid creature of God to be one with him, and reign with him over these fair possessions; and of hopelessness at the thought that anything so perfect could be accomplished in this imperfect world.

He turned immediately and walked beside her, and they both knew, in the silence that followed, that the crisis had come.

"Mistress Isabel," he said, still looking down as he spoke, and his voice sounded odd to her ears, "I wonder if you know what I would say to you."

There came no sound from her, but the rustle of her dress.

"But I must say it," he went on, "follow what may. It is this. I love you dearly."

Her walk faltered beside him, and it seemed as if she would stand still.

"A moment," he said, and he lifted his white restrained face. "I ask you to be patient with me. Perhaps I need not say that I have never said this to any woman before; but more, I have never even thought it. I do not know how to speak, nor what I should say; beyond this, that since I first met you at the door across there, a year ago, you have taught me ever since what love means; and now I am come to you, as to my dear mistress, with my lesson learnt."

They were standing together now; he was still turned a little away from her, and dared not lift his eyes to her face again. Then of a sudden he felt her hand on his arm for a moment, and he looked up, and saw her eyes all swimming with sorrow.

"Dear friend," she said quite simply, "it is impossible—Ah! what can I say?"

"Give me a moment more," he said; and they walked on slowly. "I know what presumption this is; but I will not spin phrases about that. Nor do I ask what is impossible; but I will only ask leave to teach you in my turn what love means."

"Oh! that is the hardest of all to say," she said, "but I know already."

He did not quite understand, and glanced at her a moment.

"I once loved too," she whispered. He drew a sharp breath.

"Forgive me," he said, "I forced that from you."

"You are never anything but courteous and kind," she said, "and that makes this harder than all."

They walked in silence half a dozen steps.

"Have I distressed you?" he asked, glancing at her again.

Then she looked full in his face, and her eyes were overflowing.

"I am grieved for your sorrow," she said, "and at my own unworthiness, you know that?"

"I know that you are now and always will be my dear mistress and queen."

His voice broke altogether as he ended, and he bent and took her hand delicately in his own, as if it were royal, and kissed it. Then she gave a great sob and slipped away through the opening in the clipped hedge; and he was left alone with the dusk and his sorrow.

A week later Anthony and Isabel were saying good-bye to him in the early summer morning: the pack-horses had started on before, and there were just the two saddle-horses at the low oak door, with the servants' behind. When Mr. Buxton had put Isabel into the saddle, he held her hand for a moment; Anthony was mounting behind.

"Mistress Isabel," he whispered; "forgive me; but I find I cannot take your answer; you will remember that."

She shook her head without speaking, but dared not even look into his eyes; though she turned her head as she rode out of the gates for a last look at the peaked gables and low windows of the house where she had been so happy. There was still the dark figure motionless against the pale oak door.

"Oh, Anthony!" she whispered brokenly, "our Lord asks very much."

CHAPTER VII
NORTHERN RELIGION

The Northern counties were distinguished among all in England for their loyalty to the old Faith; and this was owing, no doubt, to the characters of both the country and the inhabitants;—it was difficult for the officers of justice to penetrate to the high moorland and deep ravines, and yet more difficult to prevail with the persons who lived there. Twenty-two years before the famous Lancashire League had been formed, under the encouragement of Dr. Allen, afterwards the Cardinal, whose members pledged themselves to determined recusancy; with the result that here and there church-doors were closed, and the Book of Common Prayer utterly refused. Owing partly to Bishop Downman's laxity towards the recusants, the principles of the League had retained their hold throughout the county, ever since '68, when ten obstinate Lancastrians had been haled before the Council, of whom one, the famous Sir John Southworth himself, suffered imprisonment more than once.

Anthony and Isabel then found their life in the North very different to that which they had been living at Stanfield. Near the towns, of course, precaution was as necessary as anywhere else in England, but once they had passed up on to the higher moorlands they were able to throw off all anxiety, as much as if the penal laws of England were not in force there.

It was pleasant, too, to go, as they did, from great house to great house, and find the old pre-Reformation life of England in full vigour; the whole family present at mass so often as it was said, desirous of the sacraments, and thankful for the opportunities of grace that the arrival of the priest afforded. Isabel would often stay at such houses a week or two together, while Anthony made rounds into the valleys and to the moorland villages round-about; and then the two would travel on together with their servants to the next village. Anthony's ecclesiastical outfit was very simple. Among Isabel's dresses lay a brocade vestment that might easily pass notice if the luggage was searched; and Anthony carried in his own luggage a little altar-stone, a case with the holy oils, a tiny chalice and paten, singing-cakes, and a thin vellum-bound Missal and Ritual in one volume, containing the order of mass, a few votive masses, and the usual benedictions for holy-water, rue and the like, and the occasional offices.

In this manner they first visited many of the famous old Lancashire houses, some of which still stand, Borwick Hall, Hall-i'-the-Wood, Lydiate Hall, Thurnham, Blainscow, where Campion had once been so nearly taken, and others, all of which were provided with secret hiding-places for the escape of the priest, should a sudden alarm be raised. In none of them, however, did he find the same elaboration of device as at Stanfield Place.

First, however, they went to Speke Hall, the home of Mr. Norreys, on the banks of the Mersey, a beautiful house of magpie architecture, and furnished with a remarkable underground passage to the shore of the Mersey, the scene of Richard Brittain's escape.

Here they received a very warm welcome.

"It is as I wrote to Mr. Buxton," said his host on the evening of their arrival, "in many places in this country any religion other than the Catholic is unknown. The belief of the Protestant is as strange as that of the Turk, both utterly detested. I was in Cumberland a few months back; there in more than one village the old worship goes on as it has done since Christianity first came to this island. But I hope you will go up there, now that you have come so far. You would do a great work for Christ his Church."

He told him, too, a number of stories of the zeal and constancy shown on behalf of the Religion; of small squires who were completely ruined by the fines laid upon them; of old halls that were falling to pieces through the ruin brought upon their staunch owners; and above all of the priests that Lancashire had added to the roll of the martyrs—Anderton, Marsden, and Thompson among others—and of the joy shown when the glorious news of their victory over death reached the place where they had been born or where they had ministered.

"At Preston," he said, "when the news of Mr. Greenaway's death reached them, they tolled the bells for sorrow. But his old mother ran from her house to the street when they had broken the news to her: 'Peal them, peal them!' she cried, 'for I have borne a martyr to God.'"

He talked, too, of Campion, of his sermons on "The King who went a journey," and the "Hail, Mary"; and told him of the escape at Blainscow Hall, where the servant-girl, seeing the pursuivants at hand, pushed the Jesuit, with quick wit and courage, into the duck-pond, so that he came out disguised indeed—in green mud—and was mocked at by the very officers as a clumsy suitor of maidens.

Anthony's heart warmed within him as he sat and listened to these tales of patience and gallantry.

"I would lay down my life to serve such folk," he said; and Isabel looked with deep-kindled eyes from the one to the other.

They did not stay more than a day or two at Speke Hall, for, as Mr. Norreys said, the necessaries of salvation were to be had there already; but they moved on almost at once northwards, always arriving at some central point for Saturdays and Sundays, so that the Catholics round could come in for shrift and housel. In this manner they passed up through Lancashire, and pushed still northwards, hearing that a priest was sorely needed, through the corner of Westmoreland, up the Lake country, through into Cumberland itself. At Kendal, where they stayed two nights, Anthony received a message that determined him, after consultation with Isabel, to push on as far as Skiddaw, and to make that the extreme limit of his journey. He sent the messenger, a wild-looking North-countryman, back with a verbal answer to that effect, and named a date when they would arrive.

It was already dark, two weeks later, when they arrived at the point where the guide was to meet them, as they had lost their way more than once already. Here were a couple of men with torches, waiting for them behind a rock, who had come down from the village, a mile farther on, to bring them up the difficult stony path that was the only means of access to it. The track went up a ravine, with a rock-wall rising on their left, on which the light of the torches shone, and tumbled ground, covered with heather, falling rapidly away on their right down to a gulf of darkness whence they could hear the sound of the torrent far below; the path was uneven, with great stones here and there, and sharp corners in it, and as they went it was all they could do to keep their tired horses from stumbling, for a slip would have been dangerous under the circumstances. The men who led them said little, as it was impossible for a horse and a man to walk abreast, but Anthony was astonished to see again and again, as they turned a corner, another man with a torch and some weapon, a pike, or a sword, start up and salute him, or sometimes a group, with barefooted boys, and then attach themselves to the procession either before or behind; until in a short while there was an escort of some thirty or forty accompanying the cavalcade. At last, as they turned a corner, the lighted windows of a belfry showed against the dark moor beyond, and in a moment more, as if there were a watcher set there to look out for the torches, a peal of five bells clashed out from the tower; then, as they rose yet higher, the path took a sudden turn and a dip between two towering rocks, and the whole village lay beneath them, with lights in every window to welcome the priest, the first that they had seen for eight months, when the old Marian rector, the elder brother of the squire, had died.

It was now late, so Anthony and Isabel were conducted immediately to the Hall, an old house immediately adjoining the churchyard; and here, too, the windows were blazing with welcome, and the tall squire, Mr. Brian, with his wife and children behind, was standing before the bright hall-door at the top of the steps. The men and boys that had brought them so far, and were standing in the little court with their torches uplifted, now threw themselves on their knees to receive the priest's blessing, before they went home; and Anthony blessed them and thanked them, and went indoors with his sister, strangely moved and uplifted.

The two following days were full of hard work and delight for Anthony. He was to say mass at half-past six next morning, and came out of the house a little after six o'clock; the sun was just rising to his right over a shoulder of Skiddaw, which dominated the eastern horizon; and all round him, stretched against the sky in all directions, were the high purple moors in the strange dawn-light. Immediately in front of him, not thirty yards away, stood the church, with its tower, two aisles, and a chapel on a little promontory of rock which jutted out over the bed of the torrent along which he had climbed the night before; and to his left lay the straggling street of the village. All was perfectly still except for the dash of the stream over the rocks; but from one or two houses a thin skein of smoke was rising straight into the air. Anthony stood rapt in delight, and drew long breaths of the cool morning air, laden with freshness and fragrant with the mellow scent of the heather and the autumnal smells.

He was completely taken by surprise when he entered the church, for, for the first time since he could remember, he saw an English church in its true glory. It had been built for a priory-church of Holm-Cultram, but for some reason had never been used as that, and had become simply the parish church of the village. Across the centre and the northern aisle ran an elaborate screen, painted in rich colours, and the southern chapel, which ran eastwards of the porch, was separated in a similar way from the rest of the church. Over the central screen was the great rood, with its attendant figures, exquisitely carved and painted; in every direction, as Anthony looked beyond the screens, gleamed rich windows, with figures and armorial bearings; here and there tattered banners hung on the walls; St. Christopher stood on the north wall opposite the door, to guard from violence all who looked upon him day by day; a little painting of the Baptist hung on a pillar over against the font, and a Vernacle by the pulpit; and all round the walls hung little pictures, that the poor and unlearned might read the story of redemption there. But the chief glory of all was the solemn high altar, with its riddells surmounted by taper-bearing gilded angels, with its brocade cloth, and its painted halpas behind; and above it, before the rich window which smouldered against the dawn, hung the awful pyx, covered by the white silk cloth, but empty; waiting for the priest to come and bid the Shechinah of the Lord to brood there again over this gorgeous throne beneath, against the brilliant halo of the painted glass behind.

Anthony knelt a moment and thanked God for bringing him here, and then passed up into the north aisle, where the image of the Mother of God presided, as she had done for three hundred years, over her little altar against the wall. Anthony said his preparation and vested at the altar; and was astonished to find at least thirty people to hear mass: none, of course, made their communion, but Anthony, when he had ended, placed the Body of the Lord once more in the hanging pyx and lit the lamp before it.

Then all day he sat in the north chapel, with the dash and loud thunder of the mountain stream entering through the opened panes of the east window, and the stained sunlight, in gorgeous colours, creeping across the red tiles at his feet, glowing and fading as the clouds moved over the sun, while the people came and were shriven; with the exception of an hour in the middle of the day and half an hour for supper in the evening, he was incessantly occupied until nine o'clock at night. From the upland dales all round they streamed in, at news of the priest, and those who had come from far and were fasting he communicated at once from the Reserved Sacrament. At last, tired out, but intensely happy, he went back to the Hall.

But the next morning was yet more startling. Mass was at eight o'clock, and by the time Anthony entered the church he found a congregation of nearly two hundred souls; the village itself did not number above seventy, but many came in from the country round, and some had stayed all night in the church-porch. Then, too, he heard the North-country singing in the old way; all the mass music was sung in three parts, except the unchanging melody of the creed, which, like the tremendous and unchanging words themselves, at one time had united the whole of England; but what stirred Anthony more than all were the ancient hymns sung here and there during the service, some in Latin, which a few picked voices rendered, and some in English, to the old lilting tunes which were as much the growth of the north-country as the heather itself. The "Ave Verum Corpus" was sung after the Elevation, and Anthony felt that his heart would break for very joy; as he bent before the Body of his Lord, and the voices behind him rose and exulted up the aisles, the women's and children's voices soaring passionately up in the melody, the mellow men's voices establishing, as it seemed, these ecstatic pinnacles of song on mighty and immovable foundations.

Vespers were said at three o'clock, after baptisms and more confessions; and Anthony was astonished at the number of folk who could answer the priest. After vespers he made a short sermon, and told the people something of what he had seen in the South, of the martyrdoms at Tyburn, and of the constancy of the confessors.

"'Be thou faithful unto death,'" he said. "So our Saviour bids us, and He gives us a promise too: 'I will give thee a crown of life.' Beloved, some day the tide of heresy will creep up these valleys too; and it will bear many things with it, the scaffold and the gallows and the knife maybe. And then our Lord will see which are His; then will be the time that grace will triumph—that those who have used the sacraments with devotion; that have been careful and penitent with their sins, that have hungered for the Bread of Life—the Lord shall stand by them and save them, as He stood by Mr. Sherwin on the rack, and Father Campion on the scaffold, and Mistress Ward and many more, of whom I have not had time to tell you. He who bids us be faithful, Himself will be faithful; and He who wore the crown of thorns will bestow upon us the crown of life."

Then they sang a hymn to our Lady:

"Hail be thou, Mary, the mother of Christ,"

and the old swaying tune rocked like a cradle, and the people looked up towards their Mother's altar as they sang—their Mother who had ruled them so sweetly and so long—and entreated her in their hearts, who stood by her Son's Cross, to stand by theirs too should God ever call them to die upon one.

The next day Mr. Brian took Anthony a long walk as soon as dinner was over, across the moors towards the north side of Skiddaw. Anthony found the old man a delightful and garrulous companion, full of tales of the countryside, historical, religious, naturalistic, and supernatural. As they stood on a little eminence and looked back to where the church-tower pricked out of the deep crack in the moors where it stood, he told him the tale of the coming of the pursuivants.

"They first troubled us in '72," he said; "they had not thought it worth while before to disturb themselves for one old man like my brother, who was like to die soon; but in April of that year they first sent up their men. But it was only a pair of pursuivants, for they knew nothing of the people; they came up, the poor men, to take my brother down to Cockermouth to answer on his religion to some bench of ministers that sat there. Well, they met him, in his cassock and square cap, coming out of the church, where he had just replaced the Most Holy Sacrament after giving communion to a dying body. 'Heh! are you the minister?' say they.

"'Heh! I am the priest, if that is what you mean,' he answers back. (He was a large man, like myself, was my brother.)

"'Well, come, old man,' say they, 'we must help you down to Cockermouth.'

"Well, a few words passed; and the end was that he called out to Tim, who lived just against the church; and told them what was forward.

"Well, the pursuivants got back to Cockermouth with their lives, but not much else; and reported to the magistrates that the wild Irish themselves were little piminy maids compared to the folk they had visited that day.

"So there was a great to-do, and a deal of talk; and in the next month they sent up thirty pikemen with an officer and a dozen pursuivants, and all to take one old priest and his brother. I had been in Kendal in April when they first came—but they put it all down to me.

"Well, we were ready for them this time; the bells had been ringing to call in the folk since six of the clock in the morning; and by dinnertime, when the soldiers were expected, there was a matter of two hundred men, I should say, some with scythes and sickles, and some with staves or shepherds' crooks; the children had been sent down sooner to stone the men all the way up the path; and by the time that they had reached the churchyard gate there was not a man of them but had a cut or a bruise upon him. Then, when they turned the corner, black with wrath, there were the lads gathered about the church-porch each with his weapon, and each white and silent, waiting for what should fall.

"Now you wonder where we were. We were in the church, my brother and I; for our people had put us there against our will, to keep us safe, they said. Eh! but I was wroth when Olroyd and the rest pushed me through the door. However, there we were, locked in; I was up in one window, and my brother was in the belfry as I thought, each trying to see what was forward. I saw the two crowds of them, silent and wrathful, with not twenty yards between them, and a few stones still sailing among the soldiers now and again; the pikes were being set in array, and our lads were opening out to let the scythes have free play, when on a sudden I heard the tinkle of a bell round the outside of the tower, and I climbed down from my place, and up again to one of the west windows; there was a fearsome hush outside now, and I could see some of the soldiers in front were uneasy; they had their eyes off the lads and round the side of the tower. And then I saw little Dickie Olroyd in his surplice ringing a bell and bearing a candle, and behind him came my brother, in a purple cope I had never set eyes on before, with his square cap and a great book, and his eyes shining out of his head, and his lips opening and mouthing out Latin; and then he stopped, laid the book reverently on a tombstone, lifted both hands, and brought them down with the fingers out, and his eyes larger than ever. I could see the soldiers were ready to break and scatter, for some were Catholics no doubt, and many more feared the priest; and then on a sudden my brother caught the candle out of Dickie's hand, blew it out with a great puff, while Dickie rattled upon the bell, and then he dashed the smoking candle among the soldiers. The soldiers broke and fled like hares, out of the churchyard, down the street and down the path to Cockermouth; the officer tried to stay them, but 'twas no use; the fear of the Church was upon them, and her Grace herself could not have prevailed with them. Well, when they let us out, the lads were all a-trembling too; for my brother's face, they said, was like the destroying angel; and I was somewhat queer myself, and I was astonished too; for he was kind-hearted, was my brother, and would not hurt a fly's body; much less damn his soul; and, after all, the poor soldiers were not to blame; and 'twas a queer cursing, I thought too, to be done like that; but maybe 'twas a new papal method. I went round to the north chapel, and there he was taking off his cope.

"'Well,' he said to me, 'how did I do it?'

"'Do it?' I said; 'do it? Why, you've damned those poor lads' souls eternally. The hand of the Lord was with you,' I said.

"'Damned them?' said he; 'nonsense! 'Twas only your old herbal that I read at them; and the cope too, 'twas inside out.'"

Then the old man told Anthony other stories of his earlier life, how he had been educated at the university and been at Court in King Henry's reign and Queen Mary's, but that he had lost heart at Elizabeth's accession, and retired to his hills, where he could serve God according to his conscience, and study God's works too, for he was a keen naturalist. He told Anthony many stories about the deer, and the herds of wild white hornless cattle that were now practically extinct on the hills, and of a curious breed of four-horned sheep, skulls of all of which species hung in his hall, and of the odd drinking-horns that Anthony had admired the day before. There was one especially that he talked much of, a buffalo horn on three silver feet fashioned like the legs of an armed man; round the centre was a filleting inscribed, "*Qui pugnat contra tres perdet duos*," and there was a cross patée on the horn, and two other inscriptions, "*Nolite extollere cornu in altu*'" and "*Qui bibat me adhuc siti'*." Mr. Brian told him it had been brought from Italy by his grandfather.

They put up a quantity of grouse and several hares as they walked across the moor; one of the hares, which had a curious patch of white between his ears like a little night-cap, startled Mr. Brian so much that he exclaimed aloud, crossed himself, and stood, a little pale, watching the hare's head as it bobbed and swerved among the heather.

"I like it not," he said to Anthony, who inquired what was the matter. "Satan hath appeared under some such form to many in history. Joachimus Camerarius, who wrote *de natura dæmonum*, tells, I think, a story of a hare followed by a fox that ran across the path of a young man who was riding on a horse, and who started in pursuit. Up and down hills and dales they went, and soon the fox was no longer there, and the hare grew larger and blacker as it went; and the young man presently saw that he was in a country that he knew not; it was all barren and desolate round him, and the sky grew dark. Then he spurred his horse more furiously, and he drew nearer and nearer to the great hare that now skipped along like a stag before him; and then, as he put out his hand to cut the hare down, the creature sprang into the air and vanished, and the horse fell dead; and the man was found in his own meadow by his friends, in a swound, with his horse dead beside him, and trampled marks round and round the field, and the pug-marks of what seemed like a great tiger beside him, where the beast had sprung into the air."

When Mr. Brian found that Anthony was interested in such stories, he told him plenty of them; especially tales that seemed to join in a strange unity of life, demons, beasts and men. It was partly, no doubt, his studies as a naturalist that led him to insist upon points that united rather than divided the orders of creation; and he told him stories first from such writers as Michael Verdunus and Petrus Burgottus, who relate among other marvels how there are ointments by the use of which shepherds have been known to change themselves into wolves and tear the sheep that they should have protected; and he quoted to him St. Augustine's own testimony, to the belief that in Italy certain women were able to change themselves into heifers through the power of witchcraft. Finally, he told him one or two tales of his own experience.

"In the year '63," he said, "before my marriage, I was living alone in the Hall; I was a young man, and did my best to fear nought but deadly sin. I was coming back late from Threlkeld, round the south of Skiddaw that you see over there; and was going with a lantern, for it would be ten o'clock at night, and the time of year was autumn. I was still a mile or two from the house, and was saying my beads as I came, for I hold that is a great protection; when I heard a strange whistling noise, with a murmur in it, high up overhead in the night. 'It is the birds going south,' I said to myself, for you know that great flocks fly by night when the cold begins to set in; but the sound grew louder and more distinct, and at last I could hear the sound as of words gabbled in a foreign tongue; and I knew they were no birds, though maybe they had wings like them. But I knew that a Christened soul in grace has nought to fear from hell; so I crossed myself and said my beads, and kept my eyes on the ground, and presently I saw my lights burning in the house, and heard the roar of the stream, and the gabbling above me ceased, as the sound of the running water began. But that night I awoke again and again; and the night seemed hot and close each time, as if a storm was near, but there was no thunder. Each time I heard the roar of the stream below the house, and no more. At last, towards the morning, I set my window wide that looks towards the stream, and leaned out; and there beneath me, crowded against the wall of the house, as I could see in the growing light, was a great flock of sheep, with all their heads together towards the house, as close as a score of dogs could pack them, and they were all still as death, and their backs were dripping wet; for they had come down the hills and swum the stream, in order to be near a Christened man and away from what was abroad that night.

"My shepherds told me the same that day, that everywhere the sheep had come down to the houses, as if terrified near to death; and at Keswick, whither I went the next market-day, they told me the same tale, and that two men had each found a sheep that could not travel; one had a broken leg, and the other had been cast; but neither had another mark or wound or any disease upon him, but that both were lying dead upon Skiddaw; and the look in the dead eyes, they said, was fit to make a man forget his manhood."

Anthony found the old man the most interesting companion possible, and he persuaded him to accompany him on several of the expeditions that he had to make to the hamlets and outlying cottages round, in his spiritual ministrations; and both he and Isabel were sincerely sorry when two Sundays had passed away, and they had to begin to move south again in their journeyings.

And so the autumn passed and winter began, and Anthony was slowly moving down again, supplying the place of priests who had fallen sick or had died, visiting many almost inaccessible hamlets, and everywhere encouraging the waverers and seeking the wanderers, and rejoicing over the courageous, and bringing opportunities of grace to many who longed for them. He met many other well-known priests from time to time, and took counsel with them, but did not have time to become very intimate with any of them, so great were the demands upon his services. In this manner he met John Colleton, the canonist, who had returned from his banishment in '87, but found him a little dull and melancholy, though his devotion was beyond praise. He met, too, the Jesuit Fathers Edward Oldcorne and Richard Holtby, the former of whom had lately come from Hindlip.

He spent Christmas near Cartmel-in-Furness, and after the new year had opened, crossed the Ken once more near Beetham, and began to return slowly down the coast. Everywhere he was deeply touched by the devotion of the people, who, in spite of long months without a priest, had yet clung to the observance of their religion so far as was possible, and now welcomed him like an angel of God; and he had the great happiness too of reconciling some who, yielding to loneliness and pressure, had conformed to the Establishment. In these latter cases he was almost startled by the depth of Catholic convictions that had survived.

"I never believed it, father," said a young squire to him, near Garstang. "I knew that it was but a human invention, and not the Gospel that my fathers held, and that Christ our Saviour brought on earth; but I lost heart, for that no priest came near us, and I had not had the sacraments for nearly two years; and I thought that it were better to have some religion than none at all, so at last I went to church. But there is no need to talk to me, father, now I have made my confession, for I know with my whole soul that the Catholic Religion is the true one—and I have known it all the while, and I thank God and His Blessed Mother, and you, father, too, for helping me to say so again, and to come back to grace."

At last, at the beginning of March, Anthony and Isabel found themselves back again at Speke Hall, warmly welcomed by Mr. Norreys.

"You have done a good work for the Church, Mr. Capell," said his host, "and God will reward you and thank you for it Himself, for we cannot."

"And I thank God," said Anthony, "for the encouragement to faith that the sight of the faithful North has given to me; and pray Him that I may carry something of her spirit back with me to the south."

There were letters waiting for him at Speke Hall, one from Mr. Buxton, urging them to come back, at least for the present, to Stanfield Place, so soon as the winter work in the north was over; and another from the Rector of the College at Douai to the same effect. There was also one more, written from a little parish in Kent, from a Catholic lady who was altogether a stranger to him, but who plainly knew all about him, entreating him to call at her house when he was in the south again; her husband, she said, had met him once at Stanfield and had been strongly attracted by him to the Catholic Church, and she believed that if Anthony would but pay them a visit her husband's conversion would be brought about. Anthony could not remember the man's name, but Isabel thought that she did remember some such person at a small private conference that Anthony had given in Mr. Buxton's house, for the benefit of Catholics and those who were being drawn towards the Religion.

The lady, too, gave him instructions as to how he should come from London to her house, recommending him to cross the Thames at a certain spot that she described near Greenhithe, and to come on southwards along a route that she marked for him, to the parish of Stanstead, where she lived. This, then, was soon arranged, and after letters had been sent off announcing Anthony's movements, he left Speke Hall with Isabel, about a fortnight later.

CHAPTER VIII
IN STANSTEAD WOODS

On the first day of June, Anthony and Isabel, with their three armed servants and the French maid behind them, were riding down through Thurrock to the north bank of the Thames opposite Greenhithe. As they went Anthony pulled out and studied the letter and the little map that Mrs. Kirke had sent to guide them.

"On the right-hand side," she wrote, "when you come to the ferry, stands a little inn, the 'Sloop,' among trees, with a yard behind it. Mr. Bender, the host, is one of us; and he will get your horses on board, and do all things to forward you without attracting attention. Give him some sign that he may know you for a Catholic, and when you are alone with him tell him where you are bound."

There were one or two houses standing near the bank, as they rode down the lane that led to the river, but they had little difficulty in identifying the "Sloop," and presently they rode into the yard, and, leaving their horses with the servants, stepped round into the little smoky front room of the inn.

A man, dressed somewhat like a sailor, was sitting behind a table, who looked up with a dull kind of expectancy and whom Anthony took as the host; and, in order to identify him and show who he himself was, he took up a little cake of bread that was lying on a platter on the table, and broke it as if he would eat. This was one of Father Persons' devices, and was used among Catholics to signify their religion when they were with strangers, since it was an action that could rouse no suspicion among others. The man looked in an unintelligent way at Anthony, who turned away and rapped upon the door, and as a large heavily-built man came out, broke it again, and put a piece into his mouth. The man lifted his eyebrows slightly, and just smiled, and Anthony knew he had found his friend.

"Come this way, sir," he said, "and your good lady, too."

They followed him into the inner room of the house, a kind of little kitchen, with a fire burning and a pot over it, and one or two barrels of drink against the wall. A woman was stirring the pot, for it was near dinner-time, and turned round as the strangers came in. It was plainly an inn that was of the poorest kind, and that was used almost entirely by watermen or by travellers who were on their way to cross the ferry.

"The less said the better," said the man, when he had shut the door. "How can I serve you, sir?"

"We wish to take our horses and ourselves across to Greenhithe," said Anthony, "and Mrs. Kirke, to whom we are going, bade us make ourselves known to you."

The man nodded and smiled.

"Yes, sir, that can be managed directly. The ferry is at the other bank now, sir; and I will call it across. Shall we say in half an hour, sir; and, meanwhile, will you and your lady take something?"

Anthony accepted gladly, as the time was getting on, and ordered dinner for the servants too, in the outer room. As the landlord was going to the door, he stopped him.

"Who is that man in the other room?" he asked.

The landlord gave a glance at the door, and came back towards Anthony.

"To tell the truth, sir, I do not know. He is a sailor by appearance, and he knows the talk; but none of the watermen know him; and he seems to do nothing. However, sir, there's no harm in him that I can see."

Anthony told him that he had broken the bread before him, thinking he was the landlord. The real landlord smiled broadly.

"Thank God, I am somewhat more of a man than that," for the sailor was lean and sun-dried. Then once more Mr. Bender went to the door to call the servants in.

"Why, the man's gone," he said, and disappeared. Then they heard his voice again. "But he's left his groat behind him for his drink, so all's well"; and presently his voice was heard singing as he got the table ready for the servants.

In a little more than half an hour the party and the horses were safely on the broad bargelike ferry, and Mr. Bender was bowing on the bank and wishing them a prosperous journey, as they began to move out on to the wide river towards the chalk cliffs and red roofs of Greenhithe that nestled among the mass of trees on the opposite bank. In less than ten minutes they were at the pier, and after a little struggle to get the horses to land, they were mounted and riding up the straight little street that led up to the higher ground. Just before they turned the corner they heard far away across the river the horn blown to summon the ferry-boat once more.

There were two routes from Greenhithe to Stanstead, the one to the right through Longfield and Ash, the other to the left through Southfleet and Nursted. There was very little to choose between them as regards distance, and Mrs. Kirke had drawn a careful sketch-map with a few notes as to the characteristics of each route. There were besides, particularly through the thick woods about Stanstead itself, innumerable cross-paths intersecting one another in all directions. The travellers had decided at the inn to take the road through Longfield; since, in spite of other disadvantages, it was the less frequented of the two, and they were anxious above all things to avoid attention. Their horses were tired; and as they had plenty of time before them they proposed to go at a foot's-pace all the way, and to take between two and three hours to cover the nine or ten miles between Greenhithe and Stanstead.

It was a hot afternoon as they passed through Fawkham, and it was delightful to pass from the white road in under the thick arching trees just beyond the village. There everything was cool shadow, the insects sang in the air about them, an early rabbit or two cantered across the road and disappeared into the thick undergrowth; once the song of the birds about them suddenly ceased, and through an opening in the green rustling vault overhead they saw a cruel shape with motionless wings glide steadily across.

They did not talk much, but let the reins lie loose; and enjoyed the cool shadow and the green lights and the fragrant mellow scents of the woods about them; while their horses slouched along on the turf, switching their tails and even stopping sometimes for a second in a kind of desperate greediness to snatch a green juicy mouthful at the side.

Isabel was thinking of Stanfield, and wondering how the situation would adjust itself; Mary Corbet would be there, she knew, to meet them; and it was a comfort to think she could consult her; but what, she asked herself, would be her relations with the master of the house?

Suddenly Anthony's horse stepped off the turf on the opposite side of the road and began to come towards her, and she moved her beast a little to let him come on the turf beside her.

"Isabel," said Anthony, "tell me if you hear anything."

She looked at him, suddenly startled.

"No, no," he said, "there is nothing to fear; it is probably my fancy; but listen and tell me."

She listened intently. There was the creaking of her own saddle, the soft footfalls of the horses, the hum of the summer woods, and the sound of the servants' horses behind.

"No," she said, "there is nothing beyond——"

"There!" he said suddenly; "now do you hear it?"

Then she heard plainly the sound either of a man running, or of a horse walking, somewhere behind them.

"Yes," she said, "I hear something; but what of it?"

"It is the third time I have heard it," he said: "once in the woods behind Longfield, and once just before the little village with the steepled church."

The sound had ceased again.

"It is some one who has come nearly all the way from Greenhithe behind us. Perhaps they are not following—but again——"

"They?" she said; "there is only one."

"There are three," he answered; "at least; the other two are on the turf at the side—but just before the village I heard all three of them—or rather certainly more than two—when they were between those two walls where there was no turf."

Isabel was staring at him with great frightened eyes. He smiled back at her tranquilly.

"Ah, Isabel!" he said, "there is nothing really to fear, in any case."

"What shall you do?" she asked, making a great effort to control herself.

"I think we must find out first of all whether they are after us. We must certainly not ride straight to the Manor Lodge if it is so."

Then he explained his plan.

"See here," he said, holding the map before her as he rode, "we shall come to Fawkham Green in five minutes. Then our proper road leads straight on to Ash, but we will take the right instead, towards Eynsford. Meanwhile, I will leave Robert here, hidden by the side of the road, to see who these men are, and what they look like; and we will ride on slowly. When they have passed, he will come out and take the road we should have taken, and he then will turn off to the right too before he reaches Ash; and by trotting he will easily come up with us at this corner," and he pointed to it on the map—"and so he will tell us what kind of men they are; and they will never know that they have been spied upon; for, by this plan, he will not have to pass them. Is that a good plot?" and he smiled at her.

Isabel assented, feeling dazed and overwhelmed. She could hardly bring her thoughts to a focus, for the fears that had hovered about her ever since they had left Lancashire and come down to the treacherous south, had now darted upon her, tearing her heart with terror and blinding her eyes, and bewildering her with the beating of their wings.

Anthony quietly called up Robert, and explained the plan. He was a lad of a Catholic family at Great Keynes, perfectly fearless and perfectly devoted to the Church and to the priest he served. He nodded his head briskly with approval as the plan was explained.

"Of course it may all be nothing," ended Anthony, "and then you will think me a poor fool?"

The lad grinned cheerfully.

"No, sir," he said.

All this while they had been riding slowly on together, and now the wood showed signs of coming to an end; so Anthony told the groom to ride fifty yards into the undergrowth at once, to bandage his horse's eyes, and to tie him to a tree; and then to creep back himself near the road, so as to see without being seen. The men who seemed to be following were at least half a mile behind, so he would have plenty of time.

Then they all rode on together again, leaving Robert to find his way into the wood. As they went, Isabel began to question her brother, and Anthony gave her his views.

"They have not come up with us, because they know we are four men to three—if, as I think, they are not more than three—that is one reason; and another is that they love to track us home before they take us; and thus take our hosts too as priests' harbourers. Now plainly these men do not know where we are bound, or they would not follow us so closely. Best of all, too, they love to catch us at mass for then they have no trouble in proving their case. I think then that they will not try to take us till we reach the Manor Lodge; and we must do our best to shake them off before that. Now the plot I have thought of is this, that—should it prove as I think it will—we should ride slower than ever, as if our horses were weary, down the road along which Robert will have come after he has joined us, and turn down as if to go to Kingsdown, and when we have gone half a mile, and are well round that sharp corner, double back to it, and hide all in the wood at the side. They will follow our tracks, and there are no houses at which they can ask, and there seem no travellers either on these by-roads, and when they have passed us we double back at the gallop, and down the next turning, which will bring us in a couple of miles to Stanstead. There is a maze of roads thereabouts, and it will be hard if we do not shake them off; for there is not a house, marked upon the map, at which they can ask after us."

Isabel did her utmost to understand, but the horror of the pursuit had overwhelmed her. The quiet woods into which they had passed again after leaving Fawkham Green now seemed full of menace; the rough road, with the deep powdery ruts and the grass and fir-needles at the side, no longer seemed a pleasant path leading home, but a treacherous device to lead them deeper into danger. The creatures round them, the rabbits, the pigeons that flapped suddenly out of all the tall trees, the tits that fluttered on and chirped and fluttered again, all seemed united against Anthony in some dreadful league. Anthony himself felt all his powers of observation and device quickened and established. He had lived so long in the expectation of a time like this, and had rehearsed and mastered the emotions of terror and suspense so often, that he was ready to meet them; and gradually his entire self-control and the unmoved tones of his voice and his serene alert face prevailed upon Isabel; and by the time that they slowly turned the last curve and saw Robert on his black horse waiting for them at the corner, her sense of terror and bewilderment had passed, her heart had ceased that sick thumping, and she, too, was tranquil and capable.

Robert wheeled his horse and rode beside Anthony round the sharp corner to the left up the road along which he had trotted just now.

"There are three of them, sir," he said in an even, businesslike voice; "one of them, sir, on a brown mare, but I couldn't see aught of him, sir; he was on the far side of the track; the second is like a groom on a grey horse, and the third is dressed like a sailor, sir, on a brown horse."

"A sailor?" said Anthony; "a lean man, and sunburnt, with a whistle?"

"I did not see the whistle, sir; but he is as you say."

This made it certain that it was the man they had seen in the inn opposite Greenhithe; and also practically certain that he was a spy; for nothing that Anthony had done could have roused his suspicions except the breaking of the bread; and that would only be known to one who was deep in the counsels of the Catholics. All this made the pursuit the more formidable.

So Anthony meditated; and presently, calling up the servants behind, explained the situation and his plan. The French maid showed signs of hysteria and Isabel had to take her aside and quiet her, while the men consulted. Then it was arranged, and the servants presently dropped behind again a few yards, though the maid still rode with Isabel. Then they came to the road on the right that would have led them to Kingsdown, and down this they turned. As they went, Anthony kept a good look-out for a place to turn aside; and a hundred yards from the turning saw what he wanted. On the left-hand side a little path led into the wood; it was overgrown with brambles, and looked as if it were now disused. Anthony gave the word and turned his horse down the entrance, and was followed in single file by the others. There were thick trees about them on every side, and, what was far more important, the road they had left at this point ran higher than usual, and was hard and dry; so the horses' hoofs as they turned off left no mark that would be noticed.

After riding thirty or forty yards, Anthony stopped, turned his horse again, and forced him through the hazels with some difficulty, and the others again followed in silence through the passage he had made. Presently Anthony stopped; the branches that had swished their faces as they rode through now seemed a little higher; and it was possible to sit here on horseback without any great discomfort.

"I must see them myself," he whispered to Isabel; and slipped off his horse, giving the bridle to Robert.

"Oh! mon Dieu!" moaned the maid; "mon Dieu! Ne partez pas!"

Anthony looked at her severely.

"You must be quiet and brave," he said sternly. "You are a Catholic too; pray, instead of crying."

Then Isabel saw him slip noiselessly towards the road, which was some fifty yards away, through the thick growth.

It was now a breathless afternoon. High overhead the sun blazed in a cloudless sky, but down here all was cool, green shadow. There was not a sound to be heard from the woods, beyond the mellow hum of the flies; Anthony's faint rustlings had ceased; now and then a saddle creaked, or a horse blew out his nostrils or tossed his head. One of the men wound his handkerchief silently round a piece of his horse's head-harness that jingled a little. The maid drew a soft sobbing breath now and then, but she dared not speak after the priest's rebuke.

Then suddenly there came another sound to Isabel's ears; she could not distinguish at first what it was, but it grew nearer, and presently resolved itself into the fumbling noise of several horses' feet walking together, twice or three times a stirrup chinked, once she heard a muffled cough; but no word was spoken. Nearer and nearer it came, until she could not believe that it was not within five yards of her. Her heart began again that sick thumping; a fly that she had brushed away again and again now crawled unheeded over her face, and even on her white parted lips; but a sob of fear from the maid recalled her, and she turned a sharp look of warning on her. Then the fumbling noise began to die away: the men were passing. There was something in their silence that was more terrible than all else; it reminded her of hounds running on a hot scent.

Then at last there was silence; then gentle rustlings again over last year's leaves; and Anthony came back through the hazels. He nodded at her sharply.

"Now, quickly," he said, and took his horse by the bridle and began to lead him out again the way they had come. At the entrance he looked out first; the road was empty and silent. Then he led his horse clear, and mounted as the others came out one by one in single file.

"Now follow close; and watch my hand," he said; and he put his horse to a quick walk on the soft wayside turf. As the distance widened between them and the men who were now riding away from them, the walk became a trot, and then quickly a canter, as the danger of the sound being carried to their pursuers decreased.

It seemed to Isabel like some breathless dream as she followed Anthony's back, watching the motions of his hand as he signed in which direction he was going to turn next. What was happening, she half wondered to herself, that she should be riding like this on a spent horse, as if in some dreadful game, turning abruptly down lanes and rides, out across the high road, and down again another turn, with the breathing and creaking and jingling of others behind her? Years ago the two had played Follow-my-leader on horseback in the woods above Great Keynes. She remembered this now; and a flood of memories poured across her mind and diluted the bitterness of this shocking reality. Dear God, what a game!

Anthony steered with skill and decision. He had been studying the map with great attention, and even now carried it loose in his hand and glanced at it from time to time. Above all else he wished to avoid passing a house, for fear that the searchers might afterwards inquire at it; and he succeeded perfectly in this, though once or twice he was obliged to retrace his steps. There was little danger, he knew now, of the noise of the horses' feet being any guide to those who were searching, for the high table-land on which they rode was a labyrinth of lanes and rides, and the trees too served to echo and confuse the noise they could not altogether avoid making. Twice they passed travellers, one a farmer on an old grey horse, who stared at this strange hurrying party; and once a pedlar, laden with his pack, who trudged past, head down.

Isabel's horse was beginning to strain and pant, and she herself to grow giddy with heat and weariness, when she saw through the trees an old farmhouse with latticed windows and a great external chimney, standing in a square of cultivated ground; and in a moment more the path they were following turned a corner, and the party drew up at the back of the house.

At the noise of the horses' footsteps a door at the back had opened, and a woman's face looked out and drew back again; and presently from the front Mrs. Kirke came quickly round. She was tall and slender and middle-aged, with a somewhat anxious face; but a look of great relief came over it as she saw Anthony.

"Thank God you are come," she said; "I feared something had happened."

Anthony explained the circumstances in a few words.

"I will ride on gladly, madam, if you think right; but I will ask you in any case to take my sister in."

"Why, how can you say that?" she said; "I am a Catholic. Come in, father. But I fear there is but poor accommodation for the servants."

"And the horses?" asked Anthony.

"The barn at the back is got ready for them," she said; "perhaps it would be well to take them there at once." She called a woman, and sent her to show the men where to stable the horses, while Anthony and Isabel and the maid dismounted and came in with her to the house.

There, they talked over the situation and what was best to be done. Her husband had ridden over to Wrotham, and she expected him back for supper; nothing then could be finally settled till he came. In the meantime the Manor Lodge was probably the safest place in all the woods, Mrs. Kirke declared; the nearest house was half a mile away, and that was the Rectory; and the Rector himself was a personal friend and favourable to Catholics. The Manor Lodge, too, stood well off the road to Wrotham, and not five strangers appeared there in the year. Fifty men might hunt the woods for a month and not find it; in fact, Mr. Kirke had taken the house on account of its privacy, for he was weary, his wife said, of paying her fines for recusancy; and still more unwilling to pay his own, when that happy necessity should arrive; for he had now practically made up his mind to be a Catholic, and only needed a little instruction before being received.

"He is a good man, father," she said to Anthony, "and will make a good Catholic."

Then she explained about the accommodation. Isabel and the maid would have to sleep together in the spare room, and Anthony would have the little dressing-room opening out of it; and the men, she feared, would have to shake down as well as they could in the loft over the stable in the barn.

At seven o'clock Mr. Kirke arrived; and when the situation had been explained to him, he acquiesced in the plan. He seemed confident that there was but little danger; and he and Anthony were soon deep in theological talk.

Anthony found him excellently instructed already; he had, in fact, even prepared for his confession; his wife had taught him well; and it was the prospect of this one good opportunity of being reconciled to the Church that had precipitated matters and decided him to take the step. He was a delightful companion, too, intelligent, courageous, humorous and modest, and Anthony thought his own labour and danger well repaid when, a little after midnight, he heard his confession and received him into the Church. It was impossible for Mr. Kirke to receive communion, as he had wished, for there were wanting some of the necessaries for saying mass; so he promised to ride across to Stanfield in a week or so, stay the night and communicate in the morning.

Then early the next morning a council was held as to the best way for the party to leave for Stanfield. The men were called up, and their opinions asked; and gradually step by step a plan was evolved.

The first requirement was that, if possible, the party should not be recognisable; the second that they should keep together for mutual protection; for to separate would very possibly mean the apprehension of some one of them; the third was that they should avoid so far as was possible villages and houses and frequented roads.

Then the first practical suggestion was made by Isabel that the maid should be left behind, and that Mr. Kirke should bring her on with him to Stanfield when he came a week later. This he eagerly accepted, and further offered to keep all the luggage they could spare, take charge of the men's liveries, and lend them old garments and hats of his own—to one a cloak, and to another a doublet. In this way, he said, it would appear to be a pleasure party rather than one of travellers, and, should they be followed, this would serve to cover their traces. The travelling by unfrequented roads was more difficult; for that in itself might attract attention should they actually meet any one.

Anthony, who had been thinking in silence a moment or two, now broke in.

"Have you any hawks, Mr. Kirke?" he asked.

"Only one old peregrine," he said, "past sport."

"She will do," said Anthony; "and can you borrow another?"

"There is a merlin at the Rectory," said Mr. Kirke.

Then Anthony explained his plan, that they should pose as a hawking-party. Isabel and Robert should each carry a hawk, while he himself would carry on his wrist an empty leash and hood as if a hawk had escaped; that they should then all ride together over the open country, avoiding every road, and that, if they should see any one on the way, they should inquire whether he had seen an escaped falcon or heard the tinkle of the bells; and this would enable them to ask the way, should it be necessary, without arousing suspicion.

This plan was accepted, and the maid was informed to her great relief that she might remain behind for a week or so, and then return with Mr. Kirke after the searchers had left the woods.

It was a twenty-mile ride to Stanfield; and it was thought safer on the whole not to remain any longer where they were, as it was impossible to know whether a shrewd man might not, with the help of a little luck, stumble upon the house; so, when dinner was over, and the servants had changed into Mr. Kirke's old suits, and the merlin had been borrowed from the Rectory for a week's hawking, the horses were brought round and the party mounted.

Mr. Kirke and Anthony had spent a long morning together discussing the route, and it had been decided that it would be best to keep along the high ridge due west until they were a little beyond Kemsing, which they would be able to see below them in the valley; and then to strike across between that village and Otford, and keeping almost due south ride up through Knole Park; then straight down on the other side into the Weald, and so past Tonbridge home.

Mr. Kirke himself insisted on accompanying them on his cob until he had seen them clear of the woods on the high ground. Both he and his wife were full of gratitude to Anthony for the risk and trouble he had undergone, and did their utmost to provide them with all that was necessary for their disguise. At last, about two o'clock, the five men and Isabel rode out of the little yard at the back of the Manor Lodge and plunged into the woods again.

The afternoon hush rested on the country as they followed Mr. Kirke along a narrow seldom-used path that led almost straight to the point where it was decided that they should strike south. In half a dozen places it cut across lanes, and once across the great high road from Farningham to Wrotham. As they drew near this, Mr. Kirke, who was riding in front, checked them.

"I will go first," he said, "and see if there is danger."

In a minute he returned.

"There is a man about a hundred yards up the road asleep on a bank; and there is a cart coming up from Wrotham: that is all I can see. Perhaps we had better wait till the cart is gone."

"And what is the man like?" asked Anthony.

"He is a beggar, I should say; but has his hat over his eyes."

They waited till the cart had passed. Anthony dismounted and went to the entrance of the path and peered out at the man; he was lying, as Mr. Kirke had said, with his hat over his eyes, perfectly still. Anthony examined him a minute or two; he was in tattered clothes, and a great stick and a bundle lay beside him.

"It is a vagabond," he said, "we can go on."

The whole party crossed the road, pushing on towards the edge of the high downs over Kemsing; and presently came to the Ightam road where it began to run steeply down hill; here, too, Mr. Kirke looked this way and that, but no one was in sight, and then the whole party crossed; they kept inside the edge of the wood all the way along the downs for another mile or so, with the rich sunlit valley seen in glimpses through the trees here and there, and the Pilgrim's Way lying like a white ribbon a couple of hundred feet below them, until at last Kemsing Church, with St. Edith's Chantry at the side, lay below and behind them, and they came out on to the edge of a great scoop in the hill, like a theatre, and the blue woods and hills of Surrey showed opposite beyond Otford and Brasted.

Here they stopped, a little back from the edge, and Mr. Kirke gave them their last instructions, pointing out Seal across the valley, which they must leave on their left, skirting the meadows to the west of the church, and passing up towards Knole beyond.

"Let the sun be a little on your right," he said, "all the way; and you will strike the country above Tonbridge."

Then they said good-bye to one another; Mr. Kirke kissed the priest's hand in gratitude for what he had done for him, and then turned back along the edge of the downs, riding this time outside the woods, while the party led their horses carefully down the steep slope, across the Pilgrim's Way, and then struck straight out over the meadows to Seal.

Their plan seemed supremely successful; they met a few countrymen and lads at their work, who looked a little astonished at first at this great party riding across country, but more satisfied when Anthony had inquired of them whether they had seen a falcon or heard his bells. No, they had not, they said; and went on with their curiosity satisfied. Once, as they were passing down through a wood on to the Weald, Isabel, who had turned in her saddle, and was looking back, gave a low cry of alarm.

"Ah! the man, the man!" she said.

The others turned quickly, but there was nothing to be seen but the long straight ride stretching up to against the sky-line three or four hundred yards behind them. Isabel said she thought she saw a rider pass across this little opening at the end, framed in leaves; but there were stags everywhere in the woods here, and it would have been easy to mistake one for the other at that distance, and with such a momentary glance.

Once again, nearer Tonbridge, they had a fright. They had followed up a grass ride into a copse, thinking it would bring them out somewhere, but it led only to the brink of a deep little stream, where the plank bridge had been removed, so they were obliged to retrace their steps. As they re-emerged into the field from the copse, a large heavily-built man on a brown mare almost rode into them. He was out of breath, and his horse seemed distressed. Anthony, as usual, immediately asked if he had seen or heard anything of a falcon.

"No, indeed, gentlemen," he said, "and have you seen aught of a bitch who bolted after a hare some half mile back. A greyhound I should be loath to lose."

They had not, and said so; and the man, still panting and mopping his head, thanked them, and asked whether he could be of any service in directing them, if they were strange to the country; but they thought it better not to give him any hint of where they were going, so he rode off presently up the slope across their route and disappeared, whistling for his dog.

And so at last, about four o'clock in the afternoon, they saw the church spire of Stanfield above them on the hill, and knew that they were near the end of their troubles. Another hundred yards, and there were the roofs of the old house, and the great iron gates, and the vanes of the garden-house seen over the clipped limes; and then Mary Corbet and Mr. Buxton hurrying in from the garden, as they came through the low oak door, into the dear tapestried hall.

CHAPTER IX
THE ALARM

A very happy party sat down to supper that evening in Stanfield Place.

Anthony had taken Mr. Buxton aside privately when the first greetings were over, and told him all that happened: the alarm at Stanstead; his device, and the entire peace they had enjoyed ever since.

"Isabel," he ended, "certainly thought she saw a man behind us once; but we were among the deer, and it was dusky in the woods; and, for myself, I think it was but a stag. But, if you think there is danger anywhere, I will gladly ride on."

Mr. Buxton clapped him on the shoulder.

"My dear friend," he said, "take care you do not offend me. I am a slow fellow, as you know; but even my coarse hide is pricked sometimes. Do not suggest again that I could permit any priest—and much less my own dear friend—to leave me when there was danger. But there is none in this case—you have shaken the rogues off, I make no doubt; and you will just stay here for the rest of the summer at the very least."

Anthony said that he agreed with him as to the complete baffling of the pursuers, but added that Isabel was still a little shaken, and would Mr. Buxton say a word to her.

"Why, I will take her round the hiding-holes myself after supper, and show her how strong and safe we are. We will all go round."

In the withdrawing-room he said a word or two of reassurance to her before the others were down.

"Anthony has told me everything, Mistress Isabel; and I warrant that the knaves are cursing their stars still on Stanstead hills, twenty miles from here. You are as safe here as in Greenwich palace. But after supper, to satisfy you, we will look to our defences. But, believe me, there is nothing to fear."

He spoke with such confidence and cheerfulness that Isabel felt her fears melting, and before supper was over she was ashamed of them, and said so.

"Nay, nay," said Mr. Buxton, "you shall not escape. You shall see every one of them for yourself. Mistress Corbet, do you not think that just?"

"You need a little more honest worldliness, Isabel," said Mary. "I do not hesitate to say that I believe God saves the priests that have the best hiding-holes. Now that is not profane, so do not look at me like that."

"It is the plainest sense," said Anthony, smiling at them both.

They went the round of them all with candles, and Anthony refreshed his memory; they visited the little one in the chapel first, then the cupboard and portrait-door at the top of the corridor, the chamber over the fireplace in the hall, and lastly, in the wooden cellar-steps they lifted the edge of the fifth stair from the bottom, so that its front and the top of the stair below it turned on a hinge and dropped open, leaving a black space behind: this was the entrance to the passage that led beneath the garden to the garden-house on the far side of the avenue.

Mistress Corbet wrinkled her nose at the damp earthy smell that breathed out of the dark.

"I am glad I am not a priest," she said. "And I would sooner be buried dead than alive. And there is a rat there that sorely needs burying."

"My dear lady!" cried the contriver of the passage indignantly, "her Grace might sleep there herself and take no harm. There is not even the whisker of a rat."

"It is not the whisker that I mind," said Mary, "it is the rest of him."

Mr. Buxton immediately set his taper down and climbed in.

"You shall see," he said, "and I in my best satin too!"

He was inside the stairs now and lying on his back on the smooth board that backed them. He sidled himself slowly along towards the wall.

"Press the fourth brick of the fourth row," he said.

"You remember, Father Anthony?"

He had reached now what seemed to be the brick wall against which the ends of the stairs rested; and that closed that end of the cellars altogether. Anthony leaned in with a candle, and saw how that part of the wall against his friend's right side slowly turned into the dark as the fourth brick was pressed, and a little brick-lined passage appeared beyond. Mr. Buxton edged himself sideways into the passage, and then stood nearly upright. It was an excellent contrivance. Even if the searchers should find the chamber beneath the stairs, which was unlikely, they would never suspect that it was only a blind to a passage beyond. The door into the passage consisted of a strong oaken door disguised on the outside by a facing of brick-slabs; all the hinges were within.

"As sweet as a flower," said the architect, looking about him. His voice rang muffled and hollow.

"Then the friends have removed the corpse," said Mary, putting her head in, "while you were opening the door. There! come out; you will take cold. I believe you."

"Are you satisfied?" said Mr. Buxton to Isabel, as they went upstairs again.

"What are your outer defences?" asked Mary, before Isabel could answer.

"You shall see the plan in the hall," said Mr. Buxton.

He took down the frame that held the plan of the house, and showed them the outer doors. There was first the low oak front door on the north, opening on to the little court; this was immensely strong and would stand battering. Then on the same side farther east, within the stable-court, there was the servants' door, protected by chains, and an oak bolt that ran across. On the extreme east end of the house there was a door opening into the garden from the withdrawing-room, the least strong of all; there was another on the south side, opposite the front door—that gave on to the garden; and lastly there was an entrance into the priests' end of the house, at the extreme west, from the little walled garden where Anthony had meditated years ago. This walled garden had a very strong door of its own opening on to the lane between the church and the house.

"But there are only three ways out, really," said Mr. Buxton, "for the garden walls are high and strong. There is the way of the walled garden; the iron-gates across the drive; and through the stable-yard on to the field-path to East Maskells. All the other gates are kept barred; and indeed I scarcely know where the keys are."

"I am bewildered," said Mary.

"Shall we go round?" he asked.

"To-morrow," said Mary; "I am tired to-night, and so is this poor child. Come, we will go to bed."

Anthony soon went too. Both he and Isabel were tired with the journey and the strain of anxiety, and it was a keen joy to him to be back again in his own dear room, with the tapestry of St. Thomas of Aquin and St. Clare opposite the bed, and the wide curtained bow-window which looked out on the little walled garden.

Mr. Buxton was left alone in the great hall below with the two tapers burning, and the starlight with all the suffused glow of a summer night making the arms glimmer in the tall windows that looked south. Lower, the windows were open, and the mellow scents of the June roses, and of the sweet-satyrian and lavender poured in; the night was very still, but the faintest breath came from time to time across the meadows and rustled in the stiff leaves with the noise of a stealthy movement.

"I will look round," said Mr. Buxton to himself.

He stepped out immediately into the garden by the hall door, and turned to the east, passing along the lighted windows. His step sounded on the tiles, and a face looked out swiftly from Isabel's room overhead; but his figure was plain in the light from the windows as he came out round the corner; and the face drew back. He crossed the east end of the house, and went through a little door into the stable-yard, locking it after him. In the kennels in the corner came a movement, and a Danish hound came out silently into the cage before her house, and stood up, like a slender grey ghost, paws high up in the bars, and whimpered softly to her lord. He quieted her, and went to the door in the yard that opened on to the field-path to East Maskells, unbarred it and stepped through. There was a dry ditch on his left, where nettles quivered in the stirring air; and a heavy clump of bushes rose beyond, dark and impenetrable. Mr. Buxton stared straight at these a moment or two, and then out towards East Maskells. There lay his own meadows, and the cattle and horses secure and sleeping. Then he stepped back again; barred the door and walked up through the stable-yard into the front court. There the great iron gates rose before him, diaphanous-looking and flimsy in the starlight. He went up to them and shook them; and a loose shield jangled fiercely overhead. Then he peered through, holding the bars, and saw the familiar patch of grass beyond the gravel sweep, and the dark cottages over the way. Then he made his way back to the front door, unlocked it with his private key, passed through the hall, through a parlour or two into the lower floor of the priests' quarters; unlocked softly the little door into the walled garden, and went out on tip-toe once more. Even as he went, Anthony's light overhead went out. Mr. Buxton went to the garden door, unfastened it, and stepped out into the road. Above him on his left rose up the chancel of the parish church, the roofs crowded behind; and immediately in front was the high-raised churchyard, with the tall irregular wall and the trees above all, blotting out the stars.

Then he came back the same way, fastening the doors as he passed, and reached the hall, where the tapers still burned. He blew out one and took the other.

"I suppose I am a fool," he said; "the lad is as safe as in his mother's arms." And he went upstairs to bed.

Mary Corbet rose late next morning, and when she came down at last found the others in the garden. She joined them as they walked in the little avenue.

"Have not the priest-hunters arrived?" she asked. "What are they about? And you, dear Isabel, how did you sleep?"

Isabel looked a little heavy-eyed. "I did not sleep well," she said.

"I fear I disturbed her," said Mr. Buxton. "She heard me as I went round the house."

"Why did you go round the house?" asked Anthony.

"I often do," he said shortly.

"And there was no one?" asked Mary.

"There was no one."

"And what would you have done if there had been?"

"Yes," said Anthony, "what would you have done to warn us all?"

Mr. Buxton considered.

"I should have rung the alarm, I think," he said.

"But I did not know you had one," said Mary.

Mr. Buxton pointed to a turret peeping between two high gables, above his own room.

"And what does it sound like?"

"It is deep, and has a dash of sourness or shrillness in it. I cannot describe it. Above all, it is marvellous loud."

"Then, if we hear it, we shall know the priest-hunters are on us?" asked Mary. Mr. Buxton bowed.

"Or that the house is afire," he said, "or that the French or Spanish are landed."

To tell the truth, he was just slightly uneasy. Isabel had been far more silent than he had ever known her, and her nerves were plainly at an acute tension; she started violently even now, when a servant came out between two yew-hedges to call Mr. Buxton in. Her alarm had affected him, and besides, he knew something of the extraordinary skill and patience of Walsingham's agents, and even the story of the ferry had startled him. Could it really be, he had wondered as he tossed to and fro in the hot night, that this innocent priest had thrown off his pursuers so completely as had appeared? In the morning he had sent down a servant to the inn to inquire whether anything had been seen or heard of a disquieting nature; now the servant had come to tell him, as he had ordered, privately. He went with the man in through the hall-door, leaving the others to walk in the avenue, and then faced him.

"Well?" he said sharply.

"No, sir, there is nothing. There is a party there travelling on to Brighthelmstone this afternoon, and four drovers who came in last night, sir; and two gentlemen travelling across country; but they left early this morning."

"They left, you say?"

"They left at eight o'clock, sir."

Mr. Buxton's attention was attracted to these two gentlemen.

"Go and find out where they came from," he said, "and let me know after dinner."

The man bowed and left the room, and almost immediately the dinner-bell rang.

Mary was frankly happy; she loved to be down here in this superb weather with her friends; she enjoyed this beautiful house with its furniture and pictures, and even took a certain pleasure in the hiding-holes themselves; although in this case she was satisfied they would not be needed. She had heard the tale of the Stanstead woods, and had no shadow of doubt but that the searchers, if, indeed, they were searchers at all, were baffled. So at dinner she talked exactly as usual; and the cloud of slight discomfort that still hung over Isabel grew lighter and lighter as she listened. The windows of the hall were flung wide, and the warm summer air poured from the garden into the cool room with its polished floor, and table decked with roses in silver bowls, with its grave tapestries stirring on the walls behind the grim visors and pikes that hung against them.

The talk turned on music.

"Ah! I would I had my lute," sighed Mary, "but my woman forgot to bring it. What a garden to sing in, in the shade of the yews, with the garden-house behind to make the voice sound better than it is!"

Mr. Buxton made a complimentary murmur.

"Thank you," she said, "Master Anthony, you are wool-gathering."

"Indeed not," he said, "but I was thinking where I had seen a lute. Ah! it is in the little west parlour."

"A lute!" cried Mary. "Ah! but I have no music; and I have not the courage to sing the only song I know, over and over again."

"But there is music too," said Anthony.

Mary clapped her hands.

"When dinner is over," she said, "you and I will go to find it."

Dinner was over at last, and the four rose.

"Come," said Mary; while Isabel turned into the garden and Mr. Buxton went to his room. "We will be with you presently," she cried after Isabel.

Then the two went together to the little west parlour, oak-panelled, with a wide fireplace with the logs in their places, and the latticed windows with their bottle-end glass, looking upon the walled garden. Anthony stood on a chair and opened the top window, letting a flood of summer noises into the room.

They found the lute music, written over its six lines with the queer F's and double F's and numerals—all Hebrew to Anthony, but bursting and blossoming with delicate melodies to Mary's eyes. Then she took up the lute, and tuned it on her knee, still sitting in a deep lounging-chair, with her buckled feet before her; while Anthony sat opposite and watched her supple flashing fingers busy among the strings, and her grave abstracted look as she listened critically. Then she sounded the strings in little rippling chords.

"Ah! it is a sweet old lute," she said. "Put the music before me."

Anthony propped it on a chair.

"Is that the right side up?" he asked.

Mary smiled and nodded, still looking at the music.

"Now then," she said, and began the prelude.

Anthony threw himself back in his chair as the delicate tinkling began to pour out and overscore the soft cooing of a pigeon on the roofs somewhere and the murmur of bees through the open window. It was an old precise little love-song from Italy, with a long prelude, suggesting by its tender minor chords true and restrained love, not passionate but tender, not despairing but melancholy; it was a love that had for its symbols not the rose and the lily, but the lavender and thyme—acrid in its sweetness. The prelude had climbed up by melodious steps to the keynote, and was now rippling down again after its aspirations.

Mary stirred herself.

Ah! now the voice would come in the last chord——when all the music was first drowned and then ceased, as with crash after crash a great bell, sonorous and piercing, began to sound from overhead.

CHAPTER X
THE PASSAGE TO THE GARDEN-HOUSE

The two looked at one another with parted lips, but without a word. Then both rose simultaneously. Then the bell jangled and ceased; and a crowd of other noises began; there were shouts, tramplings of hoofs in the court; shrill voices came over the wall; then a scream or two. Mary sprang to the door and opened it, and stood there listening.

Then from the interior of the house came an indescribable din, tramplings of feet and shouts of anger; then violent blows on woodwork. It came nearer in a moment of time, as a tide comes in over flat sands, remorselessly swift. Then Mary with one movement was inside again, and had locked the door and drawn the bolt.

"Up there," she said, "it is the only way—they are outside," and she pointed to the chimney.

Anthony began to remonstrate. It was intolerable, he felt, to climb up the chimney like a hunted cat, and he began a word or two. But Mary seized his arm.

"You must not be caught," she said, "there are others"; and there came a confused battering and trampling outside. She pushed him towards the chimney. Then decision came to him, and he bent his head and stepped upon the logs laid upon the ashes, crushing them down.

"Ah! go," said Mary's voice behind him, as the door began to bulge and creak. There was plainly a tremendous struggle in the little passage outside.

Anthony threw his hands up and felt a high ledge in the darkness, gripped it with his hands and made a huge effort combined of a tug and a spring; his feet rapped sharply for a moment or two on the iron fireplate; and then his knee reached the ledge and he was up. He straightened himself on the ledge, stood upright and looked down; two white hands with rings on them were lifting the logs and drawing them out from the ashes, shaking them and replacing them by others from the wood-basket; and all deliberately, as if laying a fire. Then her voice came up to him, hushed but distinct.

"Go up quickly. I will feign to be burning papers; there will be smoke, but no sparks. It is green wood."

Anthony again felt above him, and found two iron half-rings in the chimney, one above the other; he was in semi-darkness here, but far above there was a patch of pale smoky light; and all the chimney seemed full of a murmurous sound. He tugged at the rings and found them secure, and drew himself up steadily by the higher one, until his knee struck the lower; then with a great effort he got his knee upon it, then his left foot, and again straightened himself. Then, as he felt in the darkness once more, he found a system of rings, one above the other, up the side of the chimney, by which it was not hard to climb. As he went up he began to perceive a sharp acrid smell, his eyes smarted and he closed them, but his throat burned; he climbed fiercely; and then suddenly saw immediately below him another hearth; he was looking over the fireplate of some other room. In a moment more he thrust his head over, and drew a long breath of clear air; then he listened intently. From below still came a murmur of confusion; but in this room all was quiet. He began to think frantically. He could not remain in the chimney, it was hopeless; they would soon light fires, he knew, in all the chimneys, and bring him down. What room was this? He was bewildered and could not remember. But at least he would climb into it and try to escape. In a moment more he had lifted himself over the fireplate and dropped safely on to the hearth of his own bedroom.

The fresh air and the familiarity of the room, as he looked round, swept the confusion out of his brain like a breeze. The thundering and shouting continued below. Then he went on tip-toe to the door and opened it. Round to the right was the head of the stairs which led straight into the little passage where the struggle was going on. He could hear Robert's voice in the din; plainly there was no way down the stairs. To the left was the passage that ended in a window, with the chapel door at the left and the false shelves on the right. He hesitated a moment between the two hiding-places, and then decided for the cupboard; there was a clean doublet there; his own was one black smear of soot, and as he thought of it, he drew off his sooty shoes. His hose were fortunately dark. He stepped straight out of the door, leaving it just ajar. Even as he left it there was a thunder of footsteps on the stairs, and he was at the shelves in a moment, catching a glimpse through the window on his left of the front court crowded with men and horses. He had opened and shut the secret door three or four times the evening before, and his hands closed almost instinctively on the two springs that must be worked simultaneously. He made the necessary movement, and the shelves with the wall behind it softly slid open and he sprang in. But as he closed it he heard one of the two books drop, and an exclamation from the passage he had just left; then quick steps from the head of the stairs; the steps clattered past the door and into the chapel opposite and stopped.

Anthony felt about him in the darkness, found the doublet and lifted it off the nail; slipped off his own, tearing his ruff as he did so; and then quickly put on the other. He had no shoes; but that would not be so noticeable. He had not seriously thought of the possibility of escaping through the portrait-door, as he felt sure the house would be overrun by now; but he put his eyes to the pinholes and looked out; and to his astonishment saw that the gallery was empty. There it lay, with its Flemish furniture on the right and its row of windows on the left, and all as tranquil as if there were no fierce tragedy of terror and wrath raging below. Again decision came to him; by a process of thought so swift that it was an intuition, he remembered that the fall of the book outside would concentrate attention on that corner; it could not be long before the shelves were broken in, and if he did not escape now there would be no possibility later. Then he unslid the inside bolt, and the portrait swung open; he closed it behind, and sped on silent shoeless feet down the polished floor of the gallery.

Of course the great staircase was hopeless. The hall would be seething with men. But there was just a chance through the servants' quarters. He dashed past the head of the stairs, catching a glimpse of heads and sparkles of steel over the banisters, and through the half-opened door at the end, finding himself in the men's corridor that was a continuation of the gallery he had left. On his left rose the head of the back-stairs, that led first with a double flight to the offices, the pantry, the buttery and the kitchen, and than, lower still, a single third flight down to the cellar.

He looked down the stairs; at the bottom of the first double flight were a couple of maids, screaming and white-faced, leaning and pressing against the door, immediately below the one he had just come through himself. The door was plainly barred as well, for it was now thudding and cracking with blows that were being showered upon it from the other side. The maids, it seemed to him, in a panic had locked the door; but that panic might be his salvation. He dashed down the stairs; the maids screamed louder than ever when they saw this man, whom they did not recognise, with blackened face and hands come in noiseless leaps down towards them; but Anthony put his finger on his lips as he flew past them; then he dashed open the little door that shut off the cellar-flight, closed it behind him, and was immediately in the dark.

Then he groped his way down, feeling the rough brick wall as he went, till he reached the floor of the cellar. The air was cool and damp here, and it refreshed him, for he was pouring with sweat. The noise, too, and confusion which, during his flight, had been reverberating through the house with a formidable din, now only reached him as a far-away murmur.

As he counted the four steps up, and then lifted the overhanging edge, there came upon him irresistibly the contrast between the serene party here last night, with their tapers and their delicate dresses and Mary's cool clear-clipped voice—and his own soot-stained person, his desperate energy and his quick panting and heart-beating. Then the steps dropped and he slid in; lifted them again as he lay on his back, and heard the spring catch as they closed. Then he was in silence, too, and comparative safety. But he dared not rest yet, and edged himself along as he had seen Mr. Buxton do last night. Which brick was it? "The fourth of the fourth," he murmured, and counted, and pressed it. Again the door pushed back, and with a little struggle he was first on his knees, and then on his feet. Then he swung the door to again behind him.

Then for the first time he rested; he leaned against the brick-lined side of the tunnel and passed his blackened hands over his face. Five minutes ago—yes—certainly not five minutes ago he was lounging in the west parlour, at the other end of the house, while Mary played the prelude to an Italian love-song.—What was she doing now? God bless her for her quick courage!—And Isabel and Buxton—where were they all? How deadly sick and tired he felt!—Again he passed his hands over his face in the pitch darkness.—Well, he must push on.

He turned and began to grope patiently through the blackness—step by step—feeling the roughness of the bricks beneath with his shoeless feet before he set them down; once or twice he stepped into a little icy pool, which had collected through some crack in the vaulting overhead; once, too, he slipped on a lump of something wet and shapeless; and thought even then of Mary's suspicions the night before. He pushed on, shivering now with cold and excitement, through what seemed the interminable tunnel, until at last his outstretched hands touched wood before him. He had not seen this end of the passage for nearly two years, and he wondered if he could remember the method of opening, and gave a gulp of horror at the thought that he might not. But there had been no reason to make a secret of the inside of the door, and he presently found a button and drew it; it creaked rustily, but gave, and the door with another pull opened inwards, and there was a faint glimmer of light. Then he remembered that the entrances to the tunnel at either end were exactly on the same system; and putting out his hands felt the slope of the underside of the staircase, cutting diagonally across the opening of the passage. He slid himself on to the boarding sideways, and drew the brickwork towards him till the spring snapped, and lay there to consider before he went farther.

First he ran over in his mind the construction of the garden-house.

The basement in which he was lying corresponded to the cellar under the house from which he had come, and ran the whole length of the building, about forty feet by twenty. It was a large empty chamber, where nothing of any value was kept. He remembered last time he was here seeing a heap of tiles in one corner, with a pile of disused poles; pieces of rope, and old iron in another. The stairs led up through an ordinary trap-door into what was the ground-floor of the house. This, too, was one immense room, with four latticed windows looking on to the garden, and one with opaque glass on to the lane at the back; and a great door, generally kept locked, for rather more valuable things were kept here, such as the garden-roller, flower-pots, and the targets for archery. Then a light staircase led straight up from this room to the next floor, which was divided into two, both of which, so far as Anthony remembered, were empty. Mr. Buxton had thought of letting his gardeners sleep there when he had at first built this immense useless summer-house; but he had ultimately built a little gardener's cottage adjoining it. The two fantastic towers that flanked the building held nothing but staircases, which could be entered by either of the two floors, and which ascended to tiny rooms with windows on all four sides.

When Anthony had run over these details as he lay on his back, he pushed up the stair over his face and let the front of it with the step of the next swing inwards; the light was stronger now, and poured in, though still dim, through three half-moon windows, glazed and wired, that just rose above the level of the ground outside. Then he extricated himself, closed the steps behind him, and went up the stairs.

The trap-door at the top was a little stiff, but he soon raised it, and in a moment more was standing in the ground-floor room of the garden-house. All round him was much as he remembered it; he first went to the door and found it securely fastened, as it often was for days together; he glanced at the windows to assure himself that they were bottle-glass too, and then went to them to look out. He was fortunate enough to find the corner of one pane broken away; he put his eye to this, and there lay a little lawn, with a yew-hedge beyond blotting out all of the great house opposite except the chimneys,—the house which even across the whole space of garden hummed like a hive. On the lawn was a chair, and an orange-bound book lay face down on the grass beside it. Anthony stared at it; it was the book that he had seen in Isabel's hand not half an hour ago, as she had gone out into the garden from the hall to wait until he and Mary joined her with the lute.

And at that the priest knelt down before the window, covered his face with his hands, and began to stammer and cry to God: "O God! God! God!" he said.

When Mary Corbet had seen Anthony's feet disappear, she already had the outline of a plan in her mind. To light a fire and pretend to be burning important papers would serve as an excuse for keeping the door fast; it would also suggest at least that no one was in the chimney. The ordinary wood, however, sent up sparks; but she had noticed before a little green wood in the basket, and knew that this did not do so to the same extent; so she pulled out the dry wood that Anthony had trodden into the ashes and substituted the other. Then she had looked round for paper;—the lute music, that was all. Meantime the door was giving; the noise outside was terrible; and it was evident that one or two of the servants were obstructing the passage of the pursuivants.

When at last the door flew in, there was a fire cracking furiously on the hearth, and a magnificently dressed lady kneeling before it, crushing paper into the flames. Half a dozen men now streamed in and more began to follow, and stood irresolute for a moment, staring at her. From the resistance they had met with they had been certain that the priest was here, and this sight perplexed them. A big ruddy man, however, who led them, sprang across the room, seized Mary Corbet by the shoulders and whisked her away against the wall, and then dashed the half-burnt paper out of the grate and began to beat out the flames.

Mary struggled violently for a moment; but the others were upon her and held her, and she presently stood quiet. Then she began upon them.

"You insolent hounds!" she cried, "do you know who I am?" Her cheeks were scarlet and her eyes blazing; she seemed in a superb fury.

"Burning treasonable papers," growled the big man from his knees on the hearth, "that is enough for me."

"Who are you, sir, that dare to speak to me like that?"

The man got up; the flames were out now, and he slipped the papers into a pocket. Mary went on immediately.

"If I may not burn my own lute music, or keep my door locked, without a riotous mob of knaves breaking upon me—— Ah! how dare you?" and she stamped furiously.

The pursuivant came up close to her, insolently.

"See here, my lady——" he began.

The men had fallen back from her a little now that the papers were safe, and she lifted her ringed hand and struck his ruddy face with all her might. There was a moment of confusion and laughter as he recoiled.

"Now will you remember that her Grace's ladies are not to be trifled with?"

There was a murmur from the crowded room, and a voice near the door cried:

"She says truth, Mr. Nichol. It is Mistress Corbet."

Nichol had recovered himself, but was furiously angry.

"Very good, madam, but I have these papers now," he said, "they can still be read."

"You blind idiot," hissed Mary, "do you not know lute music when you see it?"

"I know that ladies do not burn lute music with locked doors," observed Nichol bitterly.

"The more fool you!" screamed Mary, "when you have caught one at it."

"That will be seen," sneered Mr. Nichol.

"Not by a damned blind scarlet-faced porpoise!" screamed Mary, apparently more in a passion than ever, and a burst of laughter came from the men.

This was too much for Mr. Nichol. This coarse abuse stung him cruelly.

"God's blood," he bellowed at the room; "take this vixen out and search the place." And a torrent of oaths drove the crowd about the door out into the passage again.

A couple of men took Mary by the fierce ringed hands of hers that still twitched and clenched, and led her out; she spat insults over her shoulders as she went. But she had held him in talk as she intended.

"Now then," roared Nichol again, "search, you dogs!"

He himself went outside too, and seeing the stairs stamped up them. He was just in time to see the Tacitus settle down with crumpled pages; stopped for a moment, bewildered, for it lay in the middle of the passage; and then rushed at the open door on the left, dashed it open, and found a little empty room, with a chair or two, and a table—but no sign of the priest. It was like magic.

Then out he came once more, and went into Anthony's own room. The great bed was on his right, the window opposite, the fireplace to the left, and in the middle lay two sooty shoes. Instinctively he bent and touched them, and found them warm; then he sprang to the door, still keeping his face to the room, and shouted for help.

"He is here, he is here!" he cried. And a thunder of footsteps on the stairs answered him.

Meanwhile the men that held Mary followed the others along the passage, but while the leaders went on and round into the lower corridor, the two men-at-arms with their prisoner turned aside into the parlour that served as an ante-chamber to the hall beyond, where they released her. Here, though it was empty of people, all was in confusion; the table had been overturned in the struggle that had raged along here between Lackington's men, who had entered from the front door, and the servants of the house, who had rushed in from their quarters at the first alarm and intercepted them. One chair lay on its side, with its splintered carved arm beside it. As Mary stood a moment looking about her, the door from the hall that had been closed, again opened, and Isabel came through; and a man's voice said:

"You must wait here, madam"; then the door closed behind her.

"Isabel," said Mary.

The two looked at one another a moment, but before either spoke again the door again half-opened, and a voice began to speak, as if its owner still held the handle.

"Very well, Lackington, keep him in his room. I will go through here to Nichol."

Isabel had drawn a sharp breath as the voice began, and as the door opened wider she turned and faced it. Then Hubert came in, and recoiled on the threshold. There fell a complete silence in the room.

"Hubert," said Isabel after a moment, "what are you doing here?"

Hubert shut the door abruptly and leaned against it, staring at her; his face had gone white under the tan. Isabel still looked at him steadily, and her eyes were eloquent. Then she spoke again, and something in her voice quickened the beating of Mary's heart as she listened.

"Hubert, have you forgotten us?"

Still Hubert stared; then he stood upright. The two men-at-arms were watching in astonishment.

"I will see to the ladies," he said abruptly, and waved his hand. They still hesitated a moment.

"Go," he said again sharply, and pointed to the door. He was a magistrate, and responsible; and they turned and went.

Then Hubert looked at Isabel again.

"Isabel," he said, "if I had known——"

"Stay," she interrupted, "there is no time for explanations except mine. Anthony is in the house; I do not know where. You must save him."

There was no entreaty or anxiety in her voice; nothing but a supreme dignity and an assurance that she would be obeyed.

"But——" he began. The door was opened from the hall, and a little party of searchers appeared, but halted when the magistrate turned round.

"Come with me," he said to the two women, "you must have a room kept for you upstairs," and he held back the door for them to pass.

Isabel put out her hand to Mary, and the two went out together into the hall past the men, who stood back to let them through, and Hubert followed. They turned to the left to the stairs, looking as they went upon the wild confusion. Above them rose the carved ceiling, and in the centre of the floor, untouched, by a strange chance, stood the dinner-table, still laid with silver and fruit and flowers. But all else was in disarray. The leather screen that had stood by the door into the entrance hall had been overthrown, and had carried with it a tall flowering plant that now lay trampled and broken before the hearth. A couple of chairs lay on their backs between the windows; the rug under the window was huddled in a heap, and all over the polished boards were scratches and dents; a broken sword-hilt lay on the floor with a feathered cap beside it. There were half a dozen men guarding the four doors; but the rest were gone; and from overhead came tramplings and shouts as the hunt swept to and fro in the upper floors.

At the top of the stairs was Mary's room; the two ladies, who had gone silently upstairs with Hubert behind them, stopped at the door of it.

"Here, if you please," said Mary.

Before Hubert could answer, Lackington came down the passage, hurrying with a drawn sword, and his hat on his head. Isabel did not recognise him as he stopped and tapped Hubert on the arm familiarly.

"The prisoners must not be together," he said.

Hubert drew back his arm and looked the man in the face.

"They are not prisoners; and they shall be together. Take off your hat, sir."

Then, as Lackington drew back astonished, he opened the door.

"You shall not be disturbed here," he said, and the two went in, and the door closed behind them. There was a murmur of voices outside the door, and they heard a name called once or twice, and the sound of footsteps. Then came a tap, and Hubert stepped in quietly and closed the door.

"I have placed my own man outside," he said, "and none shall trouble you—and—Mistress Isabel—I will do my best." Then he bowed and went out.

The long miserable afternoon began. They watched through the windows the sentries going up and down the broad paths between the glowing flower-beds; and out, over the high iron fence that separated the garden from the meadows, the crowd of villagers and children watching.

But the real terror for them both lay in the sounds that came from the interior of the house. There was a continual tramp of the sentries placed in every corridor and lobby, and of the messengers that went to and fro. Then from room after room came the sounds of blows, the rending of woodwork, and once or twice the crash of glass, as the searchers went about their work; and at every shout the women shuddered or drew their breath sharply, for any one of the noises might be the sign of Anthony's arrest.

The two had soon talked out every theory in low voices, but they both agreed that he was still in the house somewhere, and on the upper floor. It was impossible, they thought, for him to have made his way down. There were four possibilities, therefore: either he might still be in the chimney—in that case it was no use hoping; or he was in the chapel-hole; or in that behind the portrait; or in one last one, in the room next to their own. The searchers had been there early in the afternoon, but perhaps had not found it; its entrance was behind the window shutter, and was contrived in the thickness of the wall. So they talked, these two, and conjectured and prayed, as the evening drew on; and the sun began to sink behind the church, and the garden to lie in cool shadow.

About eight there was a tap at the door, and Hubert came in with a tray of food in his hands, which he set down.

"All is in confusion," he said, "but this is the best I can do."—He broke off.

"Mistress Isabel," he said, coming nearer to the two as they sat together in the window-seat, "I can do little; they have found three hiding-holes; but so far he has escaped. I do what I can to draw them off, but they are too clever and zealous. If you can tell me more, perhaps I can do more."

The two were looking at him with startled eyes.

"Three?" Mary said.

"Yes, three—and indeed——" He stopped as Isabel got up and came towards him.

"Hubert," she said resolutely, "I must tell you. He must be still in the chimney of the little west parlour. Do what you can."

"The west parlour!" he said. "That was where Mistress Corbet was burning the papers?"

"Yes," said Mary.

"He is not there," said Hubert; "we have sent a boy up and down it already."

"Ah! dear God!" said Mary from the window-seat, "then he has escaped."

Isabel looked from one to the other and shook her head.

"It cannot be," she said. "The guards were all round the house before the alarm rang."

Hubert nodded, and Mary's face fell.

"Then is there no way out?" he asked.

Mary sprang up with shining eyes.

"He has done it," she said, and threw her arms round Isabel and kissed her.

"Well," said Hubert, "what can I do?"

"You must leave us," said Isabel; "come back later."

"Then when we have searched the garden-house—why, what is it?"

A look of such anguish had come into their faces that he stopped amazed.

"The garden-house!" cried Mary; "no, no, no!"

"No, no, Hubert, Hubert!" cried Isabel, "you must not go there."

"Why," he said, "it was I that proposed it; to draw them from the house."

There came from beneath the windows a sudden tramp of footsteps, and then Nichol's voice, distinctly heard through the open panes.

"We cannot wait for him. Come, men."

"They are going without me," said Hubert; and turned and ran through the door.

CHAPTER XI
THE GARDEN-HOUSE

During that long afternoon the master of the house had sat in his own room, before his table, hearing the ceaseless footsteps and the voices overhead, and the ring of feet on the tiles outside his window, knowing that his friend and priest was somewhere in the house, crouching in some dark little space, listening to the same footsteps and voices as they came and went by his hiding-place, and that he himself was absolutely powerless to help.

He had been overpowered in the first rush as he pealed on the alarm-bell, to which he had rushed when the groom burst in from the stable-yard crying that the outer court was full of men. Lackington had then sent him under guard to his own room, where he had been locked in with an armed constable to prevent any possibility of escape. In the struggle he had received a blow on the head which had completely dazed him; all his resource left him; and he had no desire even to move from his chair.

Now he sat, with his head on his breast, and his mind going the ceaseless round of all the possible places where Anthony might be. Little scenes, too, of startling vividness moved before him, as he sat there with half-closed eyes—scenes of the imagined arrest—the scuffle as the portrait was torn away and Anthony burst out in one last desperate attempt to escape. He saw him under every kind of circumstance—dashing up stairs and being met at the top by a man with a pike—running and crouching through the withdrawing-room itself next door—gliding with burning eyes past the yew-hedges in a rush for the iron gates, only to find them barred—on horseback with his hands bound and a despairing uplifted face with pike-heads about him.—So his friend dreamed miserably on, open-eyed, but between waking and the sleep of exhaustion, until the crowning vision flashed momentarily before his eyes of the scaffold and the cauldron with the fire burning and the low gallows over the heads of the crowd, and the butcher's block and knife; and then he moaned and sat up and stared about him, and the young pursuivant looked at him half-apprehensively.

Towards evening the house grew quieter; once, about six o'clock, there were voices outside, the door from the hall was unlocked, and a heavily-built, ruddy man came in with two pikemen, locking the door behind him. They paid no attention to the prisoner, and he watched them mechanically as they went round the room, running their eyes up and down the panelling, and tapping here and there.

"The room has been searched, sir, already," said the young constable to the ruddy-faced man, who glanced at him and nodded, and then continued the scrutiny. They reached the fireplace and the officer reached up and tapped the wood over the mantelpiece half-a-dozen times.

"Here," he called, pointing to a spot.

A pikeman came up, placed the end of his pike into the oak, and leaned suddenly and heavily upon it: the steel crashed in an inch, and stopped as it met the stonework behind. The officer made a motion, the pike was withdrawn, and he stood on tip-toe and put his finger into the splintered panel. Then he was satisfied and they passed on, still tapping the walls, and went out of the other door, locking it again behind them.

An hour later there were voices and steps again, and a door was unlocked and opened, and Mr. Graves, the Tonbridge magistrate stepped in alone. He was a pale scholarly-looking man with large eyes, and a weak mouth only partly covered by his beard.

"You can go," he said nervously to the constable, "but remain outside." The young man saluted him and passed out.

The magistrate looked quickly and sideways at Mr. Buxton as he sat and looked at him.

"I am come to tell you," he said, "that we cannot find the priest." He hesitated and stopped. "We have found several hiding-holes," he went on, "and they are all empty. I—I hope there is no mistake."

A little thrill ran through the man who sat in the chair; the lethargy began to clear from his brain, like a morning mist when a breeze rises; he sat a little more upright and gripped the arms of his chair; he said nothing yet, but he felt power and resource flowing back to his brain, and the pulse in his temples quieted. Why, if the lad had not been taken yet, he must surely be out of the house.

"I trust there is no mistake," said the magistrate again nervously.

"You may well trust so," said the other; "it will be a grievous thing for you, sir, otherwise."

"Indeed, Mr. Buxton, I think you know I am no bigot. I was sent for by Mr. Lackington last night. I could not refuse. It was not my wish——"

"Yet you have issued your warrant, and are here in person to execute it. May I inquire how many of my cupboards you have broken into? And I hope your men are satisfied with my plate."

"Indeed, sir," said the magistrate, "there has been nothing of that kind. And as for the cupboards, there were but three——"

Three!—then the lad is out of the house, thought the other. But where?

"And I trust you have not spared to break down my servants' rooms, and the stables as well as pierce all my panelling."

"There was no need to search the stables, Mr. Buxton; our men were round the house before we entered. They have been watching the entrances since eight o'clock last night."

Mr. Buxton felt bewildered. His instinct had been right, then, the night before.

"The party was followed from near Wrotham," went on the magistrate. "The priest was with them then; and, we suppose, entered the house."

"You suppose!" snapped the other. "What the devil do you mean by supposing? You have looked everywhere and cannot find him?"

The magistrate shrugged his shoulders deprecatingly, as he stood and stared at the angry man.

"And the roofs?" added Mr. Buxton sneeringly.

"They have been thoroughly searched."

Then there is but one possible theory, he reflected. The lad is in the garden-house. And what if they search that?

"Then may I ask what you propose to destroy next, Mr. Graves?"

He saw that this tone was having its effect on the magistrate, who was but a half-hearted persecutor, with but feeble convictions and will, as he knew of old.

"I—I entreat you not to speak to me like that, sir," he said. "I have but done my duty."

Then the other rose from his chair, and his eyes were stern and bright again and his lips tight.

"Your duty, sir, seems a strange matter, when it leads you to break into a friend's house, assault him and his servants and his guests, and destroy his furniture, in search of a supposed priest whom you have never even seen. Now, sir, if this matter comes to her Grace's ears, I will not answer for the consequences; for you know Mistress Corbet, her lady-in-waiting, is one of my guests.—And, speaking of that, where are my guests?"

"The two ladies, Mr. Buxton, are safe and sound upstairs, I assure you."

The magistrate's voice was trembling.

"Well, sir, I have one condition to offer you. Either you and your men withdraw within half an hour from my house and grounds, and leave me and my two guests to ourselves, or else I lay the whole matter, through Mistress Corbet, before her Grace." Mr. Buxton beat his hand once on the table as he ended, and looked with a contemptuous inquiry at the magistrate.

But the worm writhed up at the heel.

"How can you talk like this, sir," he burst out, "as if you had but two guests?"

"Two guests? I do not understand you. How should there be more?"

"Then for whom are the four places laid at table?" he answered indignantly.

Mr. Buxton felt a sudden desperate sinking, and he could not answer for a moment. The magistrate passed his shaking hand over his mouth and beard once or twice; but the thrust had gone home, and there was no parry or riposte. He followed it up.

"Now, sir, be reasonable. I came in here to make terms. We *know* the priest has been here. It is certain beyond all question. All that is uncertain is whether he is here now or escaped. We have searched thoroughly; we must search again to-morrow; but in the meanwhile, while you yourself must be under restraint, your guests shall have what liberty they wish; and you yourself shall have all reasonable comfort and ease. So—so, if we do not find the priest, I trust that you and—and—Mistress Corbet will agree to overlook any rashness on my part—and—and let her Grace remain in ignorance."

Mr. Buxton had been thinking furiously during this little speech. He saw the mistake he had made in taking the high line, and his wretched forgetfulness of the fourth place at table. He must make terms, though it tasted bitter.

"Well, Mr. Graves," he said, "I have no wish to be hard upon you. All I ask is to be out of the house when the search is made, and that the ladies shall come and go as they please."

The magistrate leapt at the lure like a trout.

"Yes, yes, Mr. Buxton, it shall be as you say. And to what house will you retire?"

Mr. Buxton appeared to reflect; he tapped on the table with a meditative finger and looked at the ceiling.

"It must be too far away," he said slowly, "and—and the Rector would scarce like to receive me. Perhaps in—or——Why not my summer-house?" he added suddenly.

Mr. Graves' face was irradiated with smiles.

"Thank you, Mr. Buxton, certainly, it shall be as you say. And where is the summer-house?"

"It is across the garden," said the other carelessly. "I wonder you have not searched it in your zeal."

"Shall I send a man to prepare it?" asked the magistrate eagerly. "Will you go there to-night?"

"Well, shall we go across there together now? I give you my parole," he added, smiling, and standing up.

"Indeed,—as you wish. I cannot tell you, sir, how grateful I am. You have made my duty almost a pleasure, sir."

They went out together into the hall, Mr. Buxton carrying the key of the garden-house that he had taken from the drawer of his table; he glanced ruefully at the wrecked furniture and floor, and his eyes twinkled for a moment as they rested on the four places at table still undisturbed, and then met the magistrate's sidelong look. The men were still at the doors, resting now on chairs or leaning against the wall, with their weapons beside them; it was weary work this mounting sentry and losing the hunt, and their faces showed it. The two passed out together into the garden, and began to walk up the path that led straight across the avenue to where the high vanes of the garden-house stood up grotesque and towering against the evening sky, above the black yew-hedges.

All the while they went Mr. Buxton was thinking out his plan. It was still incoherent; but, at any rate, it was a step gained to be able to communicate with Anthony again; and at least the poor lad should have some supper. And then he smiled to himself with relief as he saw what an improvement there had been in the situation as it had appeared to him an hour ago. Why, they would search the house again next day; find no one, and retire apologising. His occupancy of the garden-house with the magistrate's full consent would surely secure it from search; and he was not so well satisfied with the disguised entrance to the passage at this end as with that in the cellar.

They reached the door at last. There were three steps going up to it, and Mr. Buxton went up them, making a good deal of noise as he did so, to ensure Anthony's hearing him should he be above ground. Then, as if with great difficulty, he unlocked the door, rattling it, and clicking sharply with his tongue at its stiffness.

"You see, Mr. Graves," he said, rather loud, as he opened the door a little, "my prison will not be a narrow one." He threw the door open, gave a glance round, and was satisfied. The targets leaned against one wall, and two rows of flower-pots stood in the corner near where the window opened into the lane, but there was no sign of occupation. Mr. Buxton went across, threw the window open and looked out. There was a steel cap three or four feet below, and a pike-head; and at the sound of the latch a bearded face looked up.

"I see you have a sentry there," said Mr. Buxton carelessly.

"Ah! that is one of Mr. Maxwell's men."

"Mr. Maxwell's!" said the other, startled. "Is he in this affair too?"

"Yes; have you not heard? He came from Great Keynes this morning. Mr. Lackington sent for him."

Mr. Buxton's face grew dark.

"Ah yes, I see—a pretty revenge."

The magistrate was on the point of asking an explanation, for he felt on the best of terms again now with his prisoner, when there were footsteps outside and voices; and there stood four constables, with Nichol, Hubert Maxwell and Lackington in furious debate coming up the path behind.

They looked up suddenly, and saw the door open and the magistrate and his prisoner standing in the opening. The four constables stood waiting for further orders while their three chiefs came up.

"Now, now, now!" said Mr. Graves peevishly, "what is all this?"

"We have come to search this house, sir," said Nichol cheerfully.

"See here, sir," said Hubert, "have you given orders for this?"

"Enough, enough," said Lackington coolly. "Search, men."

The pursuivants advanced to the steps. Then Mr. Buxton turned fiercely on them all.

"See here!" he cried, and his voice rang out across the garden. "You bring me here, Mr. Graves, promising me a little peace and quietness, after your violent and unwarranted attack upon my house to-day. I have been patient and submissive to all suggestions; I leave my entire house at your disposal; I promise to lay no complaints before her Grace, so long as you will let me retire here till it is over—and now your men persecute me even here. Have you no mind of your own, sir?" he shouted.

"Really, sir——" began Hubert.

"And as for you, Mr. Maxwell," went on the other fiercely, "are you not content with your triumph so far? Cannot you leave me one corner to myself, or would your revenge be not full enough for you, then?"

"You mistake me, sir," said Hubert, making a violent effort to control himself; "I am on your side in this matter."

"That is what I am beginning to think," said Lackington insolently.

"You think!" roared Mr. Buxton; "and who the devil are you?"

"See here, gentlemen," said Mr. Nichol, "what is the dispute? Here is an empty house, Mr. Buxton tells us; and Mr. Maxwell tells us the same. Well, then, let these honest fellows run through the empty house; it will not take ten minutes, and Mr. Buxton and his friend can take the air meanwhile. A-God's name, let us not dispute over a trifle."

"Then, a-God's name, let me go to my own house," bellowed Mr. Buxton, "and these gentlemen can have the empty house to disport themselves in till doomsday—or till her Grace looks into the matter"; and he made a motion to run down the steps, but his heart sank. Mr. Graves put out a deprecating hand and touched his arm; and Mr. Buxton very readily turned at once with a choleric face!

"No, no, no!" cried the magistrate. "These gentlemen are here on my warrant, and they shall not search the place. Mr. Buxton, I entreat you not to be hasty. Come back, sir."

Mr. Buxton briskly reascended.

"Well, then, Mr. Graves, I entreat you to give your orders, and let your will be known. I am getting hungry for my supper, too, sir. It is already an hour past my time."

"Sup in the house, sir," said Mr. Nichol smoothly, "and we shall have done by then."

Then Hubert blazed up; he took a step forward.

"Now, you fellow," he said to Nichol, "hold your damned tongue. Mr. Graves and I are the magistrates here, and we say that this gentleman shall sup and sleep here in peace, so you may take your pursuivants elsewhere."

Lackington looked up with a smile.

"No, Mr. Maxwell, I cannot do that. These men are under my orders, and I shall leave two of them here and send another to keep your fellow company at the back. We will not disturb Mr. Buxton further to-night; but to-morrow we shall see."

Mr. Buxton paid no sort of further attention to him, but turned to the magistrates.

"Well, gentlemen, what is your decision?"

"You shall sleep here in peace, sir," said Mr. Graves resolutely. "I can promise nothing for to-morrow."

"Then will you kindly allow one of my men to bring me supper and a couch of some kind, and I shall be obliged if the ladies may sup with me."

"That they shall," assented Mr. Graves. "Mr. Maxwell, will you escort them here?"

Hubert, who was turning away, nodded and disappeared round the yew-hedge. Lackington, who had been talking in an undertone to the pursuivants, now went up another alley with one of them and Mr. Nichol, and disappeared too in the gathering gloom of the garden. The other two pursuivants separated and each moved a few steps off and remained just out of sight. Plainly they were to remain on guard. Mr. Buxton and the magistrate sat down on a couple of garden-chairs.

"That is an obstinate fellow, sir," said Mr. Graves.

"They are certainly both of them very offensive fellows, sir. I was astonished at your indulgence towards them."

The magistrate was charmed by this view of the case, and remained talking with Mr. Buxton until footsteps again were heard, and the two ladies appeared, with Hubert with them, and a couple of men carrying each a tray and the other necessaries he had asked for.

Mr. Buxton and the magistrate rose to meet the ladies and bowed.

"I cannot tell you," began their host elaborately, "what distress all this affair has given me. I trust you will forgive any inconvenience you may have suffered."

Both Isabel and Mary looked white and strained, but they responded gallantly; and as the table was being prepared the four talked almost as if there were no bitter suspense at three of their hearts at least. Mr. Graves was nervous and uneasy, but did his utmost to propitiate Mary. At last he was on the point of withdrawing, when Mr. Buxton entreated him to sup with them.

"I must not," he said; "I am responsible for your property, Mr. Buxton."

"Then I understand that these ladies may come and go as they please?" he asked carelessly.

"Certainly, sir."

"Then may I ask too the favour that you will place one of your own men at the door who can conduct them to the house when they wish to go, and who can remain and protect me too from any disturbance from either of the two officious persons who were here just now?"

Mr. Graves, delighted at this restored confidence, promised to do so, and took an elaborate leave; and the three sat down to supper; the door was left open, and they could see through it the garden, over which veil after veil of darkness was beginning to fall. The servants had lighted two tapers, and the inside of the great room with its queer furniture of targets and flowerpots was plainly visible to any walking outside. Once or twice the figure of a man crossed the strip of light that lay across the gravel.

It was a strange supper. They said innocent things to one another in a tone loud enough for any to hear who cared to be listening, about the annoyance of it all, the useless damage that had been done, the warmth of the summer night, and the like, and spoke in low soundless sentences of what was in all their hearts.

"That red-faced fellow," said Mary, "would be the better of some manners. (He is in the passage below, I suppose.)"

"It is scarce an ennobling life—that of a manhunter," said Mr. Buxton. ("Yes. I am sure of it.")

"They have broken your little cupboard, I fear," said Mary again. ("Tell me your plan, if you have one.")

And so step by step a plan was built up. It had been maturing in Mr. Buxton's mind gradually after he had learnt the ladies might sup with him; and little by little he conveyed it to them. He managed to write down the outline of it as he sat at table, and then passed it to each to read, and commented on it and answered their questions about it, all in the same noiseless undertone, with his lips indeed scarcely moving. There were many additions and alterations made in it as the two ladies worked upon it too, but by the time supper was over it was tolerably complete. It seemed, indeed, almost desperate, but the case was desperate. It was certain that the garden-house would be searched next day; Lackington's suspicions were plainly roused, and it was too much to hope that searchers who had found three hiding-places in one afternoon would fail to find a fourth. It appeared then that it was this plan or none.

They supped slowly, in order to give time to think out and work out the scheme, and to foresee any difficulties beyond those they had already counted on; and it was fully half-past nine before the two ladies rose. Their host went with them to the door, called up Mr. Graves' man, and watched them pass down the path out of sight. He stood a minute or two longer looking across towards the house at the dusky shapes in the garden and the strip of gravel, grass, and yew that was illuminated from his open door. Then he spoke to the men that he knew were just out of sight.

"I am going to bed presently. Kindly do not disturb me." There was no answer; and he closed the two high doors and bolted them securely.

He dared not yet do what he wished, for fear of arousing suspicion, so he went to the other window and looked out into the lane. He could just make out the glimmer of steel on the opposite bank.

"Good-night, my man," he called out cheerfully.

Again there was no answer. There was something sinister in these watching presences that would not speak, and his heart sank a little as he put-to the window without closing it. He went next to the pile of rugs and pillows that his men had brought across, and arranged them in the corner, just clear of the trap-door. Then he knelt and said his evening prayers, and here at least was no acting. Then he rose again and took off his doublet and ruff and shoes so that he was dressed only in a shirt, trunks and hose. Then he went across to the supper-table, where the tapers still burned, and blew them out, leaving the room in complete darkness. Then he went back to his bed, and sat and listened.

Up to this point he had been aware that probably at least one pair of eyes had been watching him; for, although the windows were of bottle-end glass, yet it was exceedingly likely that there would be some clear glass in them; and, with the tapers burning inside, his movements would all have been visible to either of Lackington's men who cared to put his eye to the window. But now he was invisible. Yet, as he thought of it, he slipped on his doublet again to hide the possible glimmer of his white shirt. There was the silence of the summer night about him—the silence only emphasised by its faint sounds. The house was quiet across the garden, though once or twice he thought he heard a horse stamp. Once there came a little stifled cough from outside his window; there was the silky rustle of the faint breeze in the trees outside; and now and again came the snoring of a young owl in the ivy somewhere overhead.

He counted five hundred deliberately, to compel himself to wait; and meanwhile his sub-conscious self laboured at the scheme. Then he glanced this way and that with wide eyes; his ears sang with intentness of listening. Then, very softly he shifted his position, and found with his fingers the ring that lifted the trap-door above the stairs.

There was no concealment about this, and without any difficulty he lifted the door with his right hand and leaned it against the wall; then he looked round again and listened. From below came up the damp earthy breath of the basement, and he heard a rat scamper suddenly to shelter. Then he lifted his feet from the rugs and dropped them noiselessly on the stairs, and supporting himself by his hands on the floor went down a step or two. Then a stair creaked under his weight; and he stopped in an agony, hearing only the mad throbbing in his own ears. But all was silent outside. And so step by step he descended into the cool darkness. He hesitated as to whether he should close the trap-door or not, there was a risk either way; but he decided to do so, as he would be obliged to make some noise in opening the secret doors and communicating with Anthony. At last his feet touched the earth floor, and he turned as he sat and counted the steps—the fourth, the fifth, and tapped upon it. There was no answer; he put his lips to it and whispered sharply:

"Anthony, Anthony, dear lad."

Still there was no answer. Then he lifted the lid, and managed to hold the woodwork below, as he knelt on the third step, so that it descended noiselessly. He put out his other hand and felt the boards. Anthony had retired into the passage then, he told himself, as he found the space empty. He climbed into the hole, pushed himself along and counted the bricks—the fourth of the fourth—pressed it, and pushed at the door; and it was fast.

For the first time a horrible spasm of terror seized him. Had he forgotten? or was it all a mistake, and Anthony not there? He turned in his place, put his shoulders against the door and his feet against the woodwork of the stairs, and pushed steadily; there were one or two loud creaks, and the door began to yield. Then he knew Anthony was there; a rush of relief came into his heart—and he turned and whispered again.

"Anthony, dear lad, Anthony, open quickly; it is I."

The brickwork slid back and a hand touched his face out of the pitch darkness of the tunnel.

"Who is it? Is it you?" came a whisper.

"It is I, yes. Thank God you are here. I feared— —"

"How could I tell?" came the whisper again. "But what is the news? Are you escaped?"

"No, I am a prisoner, and on parole. But there is no time for that. You must escape—we have a plan—but there is not much time."

"Why should I not remain here?"

"They will search to-morrow—and—and this end of the tunnel is not so well concealed as the other. They would find you. They suspect you are here, and there are guards round this place."

There was a movement in the dark.

"Then why think— —" began the whisper.

"No, no, we have a plan. Mary and Isabel approve. Listen carefully. There is but one guard at the back here, in the lane. Mary has leave to come and go now as she pleases—they are afraid of her; she will leave the house in a few minutes now to ride to East Maskells, with two grooms and a maid behind one of them. She will ride her own horse. When she has passed the inn she will bid the groom who has the maid to wait for her, while she rides down the lane with the other, Robert, to speak to me through the window. The pursuivant, we suppose, will not forbid that, as he knows they have supped with me just now. As we talk, Robert will watch his chance and spring on the pursuivant. As soon as the struggle begins you will drop from the window; it is but eight feet; and help him to secure the man and gag him. However much din they make the others cannot reach the man in time to help, for they will have to come round from the house, and you will have mounted Robert's horse; and you and Mary together will gallop down the lane into the road, and then where you will. We advise East Maskells. I do not suppose there will be any pursuit. They will have no horses ready. Do you understand it?"

There was silence a moment; Mr. Buxton could hear Anthony breathing in the darkness.

"I do not like it," came the whisper at last; "it seems desperate. A hundred things may happen. And what of Isabel and you?"

"Dear friend; I know it is desperate, but not so desperate as your remaining here would be for us all."

Again there was silence.

"What of Robert? How will he escape?"

"If you escape they will have nothing against Robert; for they can prove nothing as to your priesthood. But if they catch you here—and they certainly will, if you remain here—they will probably hang him, for he fought for you gallantly in the house. And he too will have time to run. He can run through the door into the meadows. But they will not care for him if they know you are off."

Again silence.

"Well?" whispered Mr. Buxton.

"Do you wish it?"

"I think it is the only hope."

"Then I will do it."

"Thank God! And now you must come up with me. Put off your shoes."

"I have none."

"Then follow, and do not make a sound."

Very cautiously Mr. Buxton extricated himself; for he had been lying on his side while he whispered to Anthony; and presently was crouched on the stairs above, as he heard the stirrings of his friend in the dark below him. There came the click of the brickwork door; then slow shufflings; once a thump on the hollow boards that made his heart leap; then after what seemed an interminable while, came the sound of latching the fifth stair into its place; and he felt his foot grasped. Then he turned and ascended slowly on hands and knees, feeling now and again for the trap-door over him— touched it—raised it, and crawled out on to the rugs. The room seemed to him comparatively light after the heavy darkness of the basement, and passage below, and he could make out the supper-table and the outline of the targets on the opposite wall. Then he saw a head follow him; then shoulders and body; and Anthony crept out and sat on the rugs beside him. Their hands met in a trembling grip.

"Supper, dear lad?" whispered Mr. Buxton, with his mouth to the other's ear.

"Yes, I am hungry," came the faintest whisper back.

Mr. Buxton rose and went on tip-toe to the table, took off some food and a glass of wine that he had left purposely filled and came back with them.

There the two friends sat; Mr. Buxton could just hear the movement of Anthony's mouth as he ate. The four windows glimmered palely before them, and once or twice the tall doors rattled faintly as the breeze stirred them.

Then suddenly came a sound that made Anthony's hand pause on the way to his mouth; Mr. Buxton drew a sharp breath; it was the noise of three or four horses on the road beyond the church. Then they both stood up without a word, and Mr. Buxton went noiselessly across to the window that looked on to the lane and remained there, listening. The horses were now passing down the street, and the noise of their hoofs grew fainter behind the houses.

Anthony saw his friend in the twilight beckon, and he went across and stood by him. Suddenly the hoofs sounded loud and near; and they heard the pursuivant below stand up from the bank opposite. Then Mary's voice came distinct and cheerful.

"How dark it is!"

The horses were coming down the lane.

CHAPTER XII
THE NIGHT-RIDE

The sound of hoofs came nearer; Anthony's heart, as he crouched below the window, ready to spring up and over when the signal was given, beat in sick thumpings at the base of his throat, but with a fierce excitement and no fear. His hands clenched and unclenched. Mr. Buxton stood back a little, waiting; he must feign to be asleep at first.

Then came suddenly a sharp challenge from the sentry.

"It is Mistress Corbet," came Mary's cool high tones, "and I desire to speak with Mr. Buxton."

The man hesitated.

"You cannot," he said.

"Cannot!" she cried; "why, fellow, do you know who I am? And I have just supped with him."

There came a sudden sound from the other side of the summer-house, and both men in the room knew that the guards in the garden were listening.

"I am sorry, madam, but I have no orders."

"Then do not presume, you hound," came Mary's voice again, with a ring of anger. "Ho, there, Mr. Buxton, come to the window."

"Be ready," he whispered to Anthony.

"Stand back, madam," said the pursuivant, "or I shall call for help."

Then Mr. Buxton threw back the window.

"Who is there?" he asked coolly. ("Stand up Anthony.")

"It is I, Mr. Buxton, but this insolent dog— —"

"Stand *back*, madam, I say," cried the voice of the guard. Then from the garden behind came running footsteps and voices; and a red light shone through the windows behind.

"Now," whispered the voice over Anthony's head sharply.

There came a loud shout from the guard, "Help there, help!"

Anthony put his hands on to the sill and lifted himself easily. The groom had slipped from his horse while Mary held the bridle, and was advancing at the guard, and there was something in his hand. The sentry, who was standing immediately under the window, now dropped his pike point forward; and as a furious rattling began at the doors on the garden side, Anthony dropped, and came down astride of the man's neck, who crashed to the ground. Then the groom was on him too.

"Leave him to me, sir. Mount."

The groom's hands were busy with something about the struggling man's neck: the shouts choked and ceased.

"You will strangle the man," said Anthony sharply.

"Nonsense," said Mary; "mount, mount. They are coming."

Anthony ran to the horse, that was beginning to scurry and plunge; threw himself across the saddle and caught the reins.

"Up?" said Mary.

"Up"; and he slung his right leg over the flank and sat up, as Mary released the bridle, and dashed off, scattering gravel.

From the direction of the church came cries and the quick rattle of a galloping horse. Anthony dashed his shoeless heels into the horse's sides and leaned forward, and in a moment more was flying down the lane after Mary. From in front came a shout of warning, with one or two screams, and then Anthony turned the corner, checking his horse slightly at the angle, saw a torch somewhere to his right, a group of scared faces, a groom and woman clinging to him on a plunging horse, and the white road; and then found himself with loose reins, and flying stirrups, thundering down the village street, with Mary on her horse not two lengths in front. The roar of the hoofs behind, and of the little shouting crowd, with the screaming woman on the horse, died behind him as the wind began to boom in his ears. Mary was looking round now, and slightly checking her horse as they neared the bottom of the long village street. In half a dozen strides Anthony came up on her right. Then the pool gleamed before them just beyond the fork of the road.

"Left!" screamed Mary through the roar of the racing air, and turned her horse off up the road that led round in a wide sweep of two miles to East Maskells and the woods beyond, and Anthony followed. He had settled down in the saddle now, and had brought his maddened horse under control; his feet were in the stirrups, but there was no lessening of the speed. They had left the last house now, and on either side the black bushes and heatherland streamed past, with the sudden gleam of water here and there under the starlight that showed the ditches and holes with which the ground on either side of the road was honeycombed.

Then Mary turned her head again, and the words came detached and sharp.

"They are after us—could not help—horses saddled."

Anthony turned his head to release one ear from the roar of the air, and heard the thundering rattle of hoofs in the distance, but even as he listened it grew fainter.

"We are gaining!" he shouted.

Mary nodded, and her teeth gleamed white in a smile.

"Ours are fresh," she screamed.

Then there was silence between them again; they had reached a little hill and eased their horses up it; a heavy fringe of trees crowned it on their right, black against the stars, and a gleam of light showed the presence of a house among them. Farther and farther behind them sounded the hoofs; then they were swaying and rocking again down the slope that led to the long flat piece of road that ended in the slope up to East Maskells. It was softer going now and darker too, as there were trees overhead; pollared willows streamed past them as they went; and twice there was a snort and a hollow thunder of hoofs as a young sleeping horse awoke and raced them a few yards in the meadows at the side. Once Anthony's horse shied at a white post, and drew in front a yard or two; and he heard for a moment under the rattle the cool gush of the stream that flowed beneath the road and the scream of a water-fowl as she burst from the reeds.

A great exultation began to fill Anthony's heart. What a ride this was, in the glorious summer night—reckless and intoxicating! What a contrast, this sweet night air streaming past him, this dear world of living things, his throbbing horse beneath him, the birds and beasts round him, and this gallant girl swaying and rejoicing too beside him! What a contrast was all this to that terrible afternoon, only a few hours away—of suspense and skulking like a rat in a sewer; in a dark, close passage underground breathing death and silence round him! An escape with the fresh air in the face and the glorious galloping music of hoofs is another matter to an escape contrived by holding the breath and fearing to move in a mean hiding-hole. And as all this flooded in upon him, incoherently but overpoweringly, he turned and laughed loud with joy.

They had nearly come to an end of the flat by now. In front of them rose the high black mass of trees where safety lay; somewhere to the right, not a quarter of a mile in front, just off the road, lay East Maskells. They would draw rein, he reflected, when they reached the outer gates, and listen; and if all was quiet behind them, Mary at least should ask for shelter. For himself, perhaps it would be safer to ride on into the woods for the present. He began to move his head as he rode to see if there were any light in the house before him; it seemed dark; but perhaps he could not see the house from here. Gradually his horse slackened a little, as the rise in the ground began, and he tossed the reins once or twice.

Then there was a sharp hiss and blow behind him; his horse snorted and leapt forward, almost unseating him, and then, still snorting with head raised and jerking, dashed at the slope. There was a cry and a loud report; he tugged at the reins, but the horse was beside himself, and he rode fifty yards before he could stop him. Even as he wrenched him into submission another horse with head up and flying stirrup and reins thundered past him and disappeared into the woods beyond the house.

Then, trembling so that he could hardly hold the reins, he urged his horse back again at a stumbling trot towards what he knew lay at the foot of the slope, and to meet the tumult that grew in nearness and intensity up the road along which he had just galloped.

There was a dark group on the pale road in front of him, twenty yards this side of the field-path that led from Stanfield Place; he took his feet from the stirrups as he got near, and in a moment more threw his right leg forward over the saddle and slipped to the ground.

He said no word but pushed away the two men, and knelt by Mary, taking her head on his knee. The men rose and stood looking down at them.

"Mary," he said, "can you hear me?"

He bent close over the white face; her hand rose to her breast, and came away dark. She was shot through the body. Then she pushed him sharply.

"Go," she whispered, "go."

"Mary," he said again, "make your confession—quickly. Stand back, you men."

They obeyed him; and he bent his ear towards the mouth he could so dimly see. There was a sob or two—a long moaning breath—and then the murmur of words, very faint and broken by gulps for breath. He noticed nothing of the hoofs that dashed up the road and stopped abruptly, and of the murmur of voices that grew round him; he only heard the gasping whisper, the words that rose one by one, with pauses and sighs, into his ear....

"Is that all?" he said, and a silence fell on all who stood round, now a complete circle about the priest and the penitent. The pale face moved slightly in assent; he could see the lips were open, and the breath was coming short and agonised.

"... *In nomine Patris*—his hand rose above her and moved cross-ways in the air—*et Filii et Spiritus Sancti. Amen.*"

Then he bent low again and looked; the bosom was still rising and falling, the shut eyes lifted once and looked at him. Then the lids fell again.

"*Benedictio Dei omnipotentis, Patris et Filii et Spiritus sancti, descendat super te et maneat semper. Amen.*"

Then there fell a silence. A horse blew out its nostrils somewhere behind and stamped; then a man's voice cried brutally:

"Now then, is that popish mummery done yet?"

There was a murmur and stir in the group. But Anthony had risen.

"That is all," he said.

CHAPTER XIII
IN PRISON

Anthony found several friends in the Clink prison in Southwark, whither he was brought up from Stanfield Place after his arrest.

Life there was very strange, a combination of suffering and extraordinary relaxation. He had a tiny cell, nine feet by five, with one little window high up, and for the first month of his imprisonment wore irons; at the same time his gaoler was so much open to bribery that he always found his door open on Sunday morning, and was able to shuffle upstairs and say mass in the cell of Ralph Emerson, once the companion of Campion, and a lay-brother of the Society of Jesus. There he met a large number of Catholics—some of whom he had come across in his travels—and he even ministered the sacraments to others who managed to come in from the outside. His chief sorrow was that his friend and host had been taken to the Counter in Wood Street.

It was a month before he heard all that had happened on the night of his arrest, and on the previous days: he had been separated at once from his friends; and although he had heard his guards talking both in the hall where he had been kept the rest of the night, and during the long hot ride to London the next day, yet at first he was so bewildered by Mary's death that what they said made little impression on him. But after he had been examined both by magistrates and the Commissioners, and very little evidence was forthcoming, his irons were struck off and he was allowed much more liberty than before; and at last, to his great joy, Isabel was admitted to see him. She herself had come straight up to the Marretts' house, both of whom still lived on in Wharf Street, though old and infirm; and day by day she attempted to get access to her brother; until at last, by dint of bribery, she was successful.

Then she told him the whole story.

"When we left the garden-house," she said, "we went straight back, and Mary found Mr. Graves in the parlour off the hall. Oh, Anthony, how she ordered him about! And how frightened he was of her! The end was that he sent a message to the stables for her horses to be got ready, as she said. I went up with her to help her to make ready, and we kissed one another up there, for, you know, we dared not make as if we said good-bye downstairs. Then we came down for her to mount; and then we saw what we had not known before, that all the stable-yard was filled with the men's horses saddled and bridled. However, we said nothing, except that Mary asked a man what—what the devil he was looking at, when he stared up at her as she stood on the block drawing on her gloves before she mounted. There were one or two torches burning in cressets, and I saw her so plainly turn the corner down towards the church.

"Then I went upstairs again, but I could not go to my room, but stood at the gallery window outside looking down at the court, for I knew that if there was any danger it would come from there.

"Then presently I heard a noise, and a shouting, and a man ran in through the gates to the stable-yard; and, almost directly it seemed, three or four rode out, at full gallop across the court and down by the church. The window was open and I could hear the noise down towards the village. Then more and more came pouring out, and all turned the corner and galloped; all but one, whose horse slipped and came down with a crash. Oh, Anthony! how I prayed!

"Then I saw Mr. Lackington"—Isabel stopped a moment at the name, and then went on again—"and he was on horseback too in the court; but he was shouting to two or three more who were just mounting. 'Across the field—across the field—cut them off!' I could hear it so plainly; and I saw the stable-gate was open, and they went through, and I could hear them galloping on the grass. And then I knew what was happening; and I went back to my room and shut the door."

Isabel stopped again; and Anthony took her hand softly in his own and stroked it. Then she went on.

"Well, I saw them bring you back, from the gallery window—and ran to the top of the stairs and saw you go through into the hall where the magistrates were waiting, and the door was shut; and then I went back to my place at the window—and then presently they brought in Mary. I reached the bottom of the stairs just as they set her down. And I told them to bring her upstairs; and they did, and laid her on the bed where we had sat together all the afternoon.... And I would let no one in: I did it all myself; and then I set the tapers round her, and put the crucifix that was round my neck into her fingers, which I had laid on her breast ... and there she lay on the great bed ... and her face was like a child's, fast asleep—smiling: and then I kissed her again, and whispered, 'Thank you, Mary'; for, though I did not know all, I knew enough, and that it was for you."

Anthony had thrown his arms on the table and his face was buried in them. Isabel put out her hand and stroked his curly head gently as she went on, and told him in the same quiet voice of how Mary had tried to save him by lashing his horse, as she caught sight of the man waiting at the entrance of the field-path, and riding in between him and Anthony. The man had declared in his panic of fear before the magistrates that he had never dreamt of doing Mistress Corbet an injury, but that she had ridden across just as he drew the trigger to shoot the priest's horse and stop him that way.

When Isabel had finished Anthony still lay with his head on his arms.

"Why, Anthony, my darling," she said, "what could be more perfect? How proud I am of you both!"

She told him, too, how they had been tracked to Stanfield—Lackington had let it out in his exultation.

The sailor at Greenhithe was one of his agents—an apostate, like his master. He had recognised that the party consisted of Catholics by Anthony's breaking of the bread. He had been placed there to watch the ferry; and had sent messages at once to Nichol and Lackington. Then the party had been followed, but had been lost sight of, thanks to Anthony's ruse. Nichol had then flung out a cordon along the principal roads that bounded Stanstead Woods on the south; and Lackington, when he arrived a few hours later, had kept them there all night. The cordon consisted of idlers and children picked up at Wrotham; and the tramp who feigned to be asleep had been one of them. When they had passed, he had given the signal to his nearest neighbour, and had followed them up. Nichol was soon at the place, and after them; and had followed to Stanfield with Lackington behind. Then watchers had been set round the house; the magistrates communicated with; and as soon as Hubert and Mr. Graves had arrived the assault had been made. Hubert had not been told who the priest was; but he had leapt at an opportunity to harass Mr. Buxton: he had been given to understand that Anthony and Isabel were still in the north.

"He did not know; indeed he did not," cried Isabel piteously.

At another time, when she had gained admittance to him, she gave him messages from the Marretts, who had kept a great affection for the lad, who had told them tales of College that Christmas time; and she told him too of the coming of an old friend to see her there.

"It was poor Mr. Dent," she said; "he looks so old now. His wife died three years ago; you know he has a city-living and does chaplain's work at the Tower sometimes; and he is coming to see you, Anthony, and talk to you."

Three or four days later he came.

Anthony was greatly touched at his kindness in coming. He looked considerably older than his age; his hair had grown thin and grey about his temples, and the sharp birdlike outline of his face and features seemed blurred and indeterminate. His creed too, and his whole manner of looking at things of faith, seemed to have undergone a similar process. The two had a long talk.

"I am not going to argue with you, Mr. Norris," he said, "though I still think your religion wrong. But I have learnt this at least, that the greatest of all is charity, and if we love the same God, and His Blessed Son, and one another, I think that is best of all. I have learnt that from my wife—my dear wife," he added softly. "I used to hold much with doctrine at one time, and loved to chop arguments; but our Saviour did not, and so I will not."

Anthony was delighted that he took this line, for he knew there are some minds that apparently cannot be loyal to both charity and truth at the same time, and Mr. Dent's seemed to be one of them; so the two talked of old times at Great Keynes, and of the folks there, and at last of Hubert.

"I saw him in the City last week," said Mr. Dent, "and he is a changed man. He looks ten years older than this time last year; I scarcely know what has come to him. I know he has thrown up his magistracy, and the Lindfield parson tells me that the talk is that Mr. Maxwell is going on another voyage, and leaving his wife and children behind him again."

Anthony told him gently of Hubert's share in the events at Stanfield, adding what real and earnest attempts he had made to repair the injury he had done as soon as he had learnt that it was his friend that was in hiding.

"There was no treachery against me, Mr. Dent, you see," he added.

Mr. Dent pecked a little in the air with pursed lips and eyes fixed on the ground; and a vision of the pulpit at Great Keynes moved before Anthony's eyes.

"Yes, yes, yes," he said; "I understand—I quite understand."

Before Mr. Dent took his leave he unburdened himself of what he had really come to say.

"Master Anthony," he said, standing up and fingering his hat round and round, "I said I talked no doctrine now; but I must unsay that; and— you will not think me impertinent if I ask you something?"

"My dear Mr. Dent——" began the other, standing and smiling too.

"Thank you, thank you—I felt sure—then it is this: I do not know much about the Popish religion, though I used to once, and I may be very mistaken; but I would like you to satisfy me before I go on one point"; and he fixed his anxious peering eyes on Anthony's face. "Can you say, Master Anthony, from a full heart, that you fix all your hope and confidence for salvation in Christ's merits alone?"

Anthony smiled frankly in his face.

"Indeed, in none other," he said, "and from a full heart."

"Ah well," and the birdlike face began to beam and twitch, "and—and there is nothing of confidence in yourself and your works—and—and there is no talk of Holy Mary in the matter?"

Anthony smiled again. He wished to avoid useless controversy.

"Briefly," he said, "my belief is that I am a very great sinner, that I deserve eternal hell; but I humbly place all my trust in the Precious Blood of my Saviour, and in that alone. Does that satisfy you?"

Mr. Dent's face was breaking into smiles, and at the end he took the priest's face in his hands and kissed him gently twice on the cheeks.

"Then, my dear boy, I fear nothing for you. May that salvation you hope for be yours." And then without a word he was gone.

Anthony's conscience reproached him a little that he had said nothing of the Church to the minister; but Mr. Dent had been so peremptory about doctrine that it was hard for the younger man to say what he would have wished. He told him, however, plainly on his next visit that he held wholeheartedly too that the Catholic Church was the treasury of Grace that Christ had instituted, and added a little speech about his longing to see his old friend a Catholic too; but Mr. Dent shook his head. The corners of his eyes wrinkled a little, and a shade of his old fretfulness passed over his face.

"Nay, if you talk like that," he said, "I must be gone. I am no theologian. You must let me alone."

He gave him news this time of Mr. Buxton.

"He is in the Counter, as you know," he said, "and is a very bright and cheerful person, it seems to me. Mistress Isabel asked me to see him and give her news of him, for she cannot get admittance. He is in a cell, little and nasty; but he said to me that a Protestant prison was a Papist's pleasaunce—in fact he said it twice. And he asked very eagerly after you and Mistress Isabel. He tried, too, to inveigle me into talk of Peter his prerogative, but I would not have it. It was Lammas Day when I saw him, and he spoke much of it."

Anthony asked whether there was anything said of what punishment Mr. Buxton would suffer.

"Well," said Mr. Dent, "the Lieutenant of the Tower told me that her Grace was so sad at the death of Mistress Corbet that she was determined that no more blood should be shed than was obliged over this matter; and that Mr. Buxton, he thought, would be but deprived of his estates and banished; but I know not how that may be. But we shall soon know."

These weeks of waiting were full of consolation and refreshment to Anthony: the nervous stress of the life of the seminary priest in England, full of apprehension and suspense, crowned, as it had been in his case, by the fierce excitement of the last days of his liberty—all this had strained and distracted his soul, and the peace of the prison life, with the certainty that no efforts of his own could help him now, quieted and strengthened him for the ordeal he foresaw. At this time, too, he used to spend two or three hours a day in meditation, and found the greatest benefit in following the tranquil method of prayer prescribed by Louis de Blois, with whose writings he had made acquaintance at Douai. Each morning, too, he said a "dry mass," and during the whole of his imprisonment at the Clink managed to make his confession at least once a week, and besides his communion at mass on Sundays, communicated occasionally from the Reserved Sacrament, which he was able to keep in a neighbouring cell, unknown to his gaoler.

And so the days went by, as orderly as in a Religious House; he rose at a fixed hour, observed the greatest exactness in his devotions, and did his utmost to prevent any visitors being admitted to see him, or any from another cell coming into his own, until he had finished his first meditation and said his office. And there began to fall upon him a kind of mellow peace that rose at times of communion and prayer to a point so ravishing, that he began to understand that it would not be a light cross for which such preparatory graces were necessary.

Towards the middle of September he received intelligence that evidence had been gathering against him, and that one or two were come from Lancashire under guard; and that he would be brought before the Commissioners again immediately.

Within two days this came about. He was sent for across the water to the Tower, and after waiting an hour or two with his gaoler downstairs in the basement of the White Tower, was taken up into the great Hall where the Council sat. There was a table at the farther end where they were sitting, and as Anthony looked round he saw through openings all round in the inner wall the little passage where the sentries walked, and heard their footfalls.

The preliminaries of identification and the like had been disposed of at previous examinations before Mr. Young—a name full of sinister suggestiveness to the Catholics; and so, after he had been given a seat at a little distance from the table behind which the Commissioners sat, he was questioned minutely as to his journey in the North of England.

"What were you there for, Mr. Norris?" inquired the Secretary of the Council.

"I went to see friends, and to do my business."

"Then that resolves itself into two heads: One, Who are your friends. Two, What was your business?"

Now it had been established beyond a doubt at previous examinations that he was a priest; a student of Douai who had apostatised had positively identified him; so Anthony answered boldly:

"My friends were Catholics; and my business was the reconciling of souls to their Creator."

"And to the Pope of Rome," put in Wade.

"Who is Christ's Vicar," continued Anthony.

"And a pestilent knave," concluded a fiery-faced man whom Anthony did not know.

But the Commissioners wanted more than that; it was true that Anthony was already convicted of high treason in having been ordained beyond the seas and in exercising his priestly functions in England; but the exacting of the penalty for religion alone was apt to raise popular resentment; and it was far preferable in the eyes of the authorities to entangle a priest in the political net before killing him. So they passed over for the present his priestly functions and first demanded a list of all the places where he had stayed in the north.

"You ask what is impossible," said Anthony, with his eyes on the ground and his heart beating sharply, for he knew that now peril was near.

"Well," said Wade, "let us put it another way. We know that you were at Speke Hall, Blainscow, and other places. I have a list here," and he tapped the table, "but we want your name to it."

"Let me see the paper," said Anthony.

"Nay, nay, tell us first."

"I cannot sign the paper except I see it," said Anthony, smiling.

"Give it him," said a voice from the end of the table.

"Here then," said Wade unwillingly.

Anthony got up and took the paper from him, and saw one or two places named where he had not been, and saw that it had been drawn up at any rate partly on guesswork.

He put the paper down and went back to his chair and sat down.

"It is not true," he said, looking steadily at the Secretary; "I cannot sign it."

"Do you deny that you have been to any of these places?" inquired Wade indignantly.

"The paper is not true," said Anthony again.

"Well, then, show us what is not true upon it."

"I cannot."

"We will find means to persuade you," said the Secretary.

"If God permits," said Anthony.

Wade glanced round inquiringly and shrugged his shoulders; one or two shook their heads.

"Well, then, we will turn to another point. There are known to have been certain Jesuit priests in Lancashire in November of last year—do you deny that, sir?"

"You ask too much," said Anthony, smiling again; "they may have been there for aught I know, for I certainly did not see them elsewhere at the time you mention."

Wade frowned, but the one at the end laughed loud.

"He has you there, Wade," he said.

"This is foolery," said the Secretary. "Well, these two, Father Edward Oldcorne and Father Holtby were in Lancashire in November; and you, Mr. Norris, spoke with them then. We wish to know where they are now, and you must tell us."

"You have yet to prove that I spoke with them," said Anthony, for the trap was too transparent.

"But we know that."

"That may or may not be; but it is for you to prove it."

"Nay, for you to tell us."

"For you to prove it."

Wade lost his temper.

"Well, then," he cried, "take this paper and see which of us is in the right."

Anthony rose again, wondering what the paper could be, and came towards the table. He saw it bore a name at the end, and as he advanced saw that it had an official appearance. Wade still held it; but Anthony took it in his hand too to steady it, and began to read; but as he read a mist rose before his eyes, and the paper shook violently. It was a warrant to put him to the torture.

Wade laughed a little.

"Why, see, Mr. Norris, how you tremble at the warrant; what will it be when you — —"

But a voice murmured "Shame!" and he stopped and stared.

Anthony passed his hand over his eyes and went back to his chair and sat down; he saw his knees trembling as he sat, and hated himself for it; but he cried bravely:

"The flesh is weak, but, please God, the spirit is willing."

"Well, then," said Wade again, "must we execute this warrant, or will you tell us what we would know?"

"You must do what God permits," said Anthony.

Wade sat down, throwing the warrant on the table, and began to talk in a low voice to those who sat next him. Anthony fixed his eyes on the ground, and did his utmost to keep his thoughts steady.

Now he realised where he was, and what it all meant. The little door to the left, behind him, that he had noticed as he came in, was the door of which he had heard other Catholics speak, that led down to the great crypt, where so many before him had screamed and fainted and called on God, from the rack that stood at the foot of the stairs, or from the pillar with the fixed ring at its summit.

He had faced all this in his mind again and again, but it was a different thing to have the horror within arm's length; old phrases he had heard of the torture rang in his mind—a boast of Norton's, the rackmaster, who had racked Brian, and which had been repeated from mouth to mouth—that he had "made Brian a foot longer than God made him"; words of James Maxwell's that he had let drop at Douai; the remembrance of his limp; and of Campion's powerlessness to raise his hand when called upon to swear— all these things crowded on him now; and there seemed to rest on him a crushing swarm of fearful images and words. He made a great effort, and closed his eyes, and repeated the holy name of Jesus over and over again; but the struggle was still fierce when Wade's voice, harsh and dry, broke in and scattered the confusion of mind that bewildered him.

"Take the prisoner to a cell; he is not to go back to the Clink."

Anthony felt a hand on his arm, and the gaoler was looking at him with compassion.

"Come, sir," he said.

Anthony rose feeling heavy and exhausted; but remembered to bow to the Commissioners, one or two of whom returned it. Then he followed the gaoler out into the ante-room, who handed him over to one of the Tower officials.

"I must leave you here, sir," he said; "but keep a good heart; it will not be for to-day."

When Anthony got to his new cell, which was in the Salt Tower, he was bitterly angry and disappointed with himself. Why, he had turned white and sick like a child, not at the pain of the rack, not even at the sight of it, but at the mere warrant! He threw himself on his knees, and bowed down till his head beat against the boards.

"O Lord Jesus," he prayed, "give me of Thy Manhood."

He found that this prison was more rigorous than the Clink; no liberty to leave the cell could possibly be obtained, and no furniture was provided. The gaoler, when he had brought up his dinner, asked whether he could send any message for him for a bed. Anthony gave Isabel's address, knowing that the authorities were already aware that she was a Catholic, and indeed she had given bail to come up for trial if called upon, and that his information could injure neither her nor the Marretts, who were sound Church of England people; and in the afternoon a mattress and some clothes arrived for him.

Anthony noticed at dinner that the knife provided was of a very inconvenient shape, having a round blunt point, and being sharp only at a lower part of the blade; and when the keeper came up with his supper he asked him to bring him another kind. The man looked at him with a queer expression.

"What is the matter?" asked Anthony; "cannot you oblige me?"

The man shook his head.

"They are the knives that are always given to prisoners under warrant for torture."

Anthony did not understand him, and looked at him, puzzled.

"For fear they should do themselves an injury," added the gaoler.

Then the same shudder ran over his body again.

"You mean—you mean...." he began. The gaoler nodded, still looking at him oddly, and went out; and Anthony sat, with his supper untasted, staring before him.

By a kind of violent reaction he had a long happy dream that night. The fierce emotions of that day had swept over his imagination and scoured it as with fire, and now the underlying peace rose up and flooded it with sweetness.

He thought he was in the north again, high up on a moor, walking with one who was quite familiar to him, but whose person he could not remember when he woke; he did not even know whether it was man or woman. It was a perfect autumn day, he thought, like one of those he had spent there last year; the heather and the gorse were in flower, and the air was redolent from their blossoms; he commented on this to the person at his side, who told him it was always so there. Mile after mile the moor rose and dipped, and, although Skiddaw was on his right, purple and grey, yet to his left there was a long curved horizon of sparkling blue sea. It was a cloudless day overhead, and the air seemed kindling and fresh round him as it blew across the stretches of heather from the western sea. He himself felt full of an extraordinary vitality, and the mere movement of his limbs gave him joy as he went swiftly and easily forward over the heather. There was the sound of the wind in his ears, and again and again there came the gush of water from somewhere out of sight—as he had heard it in the church by Skiddaw. There was no house or building of any kind within sight, and he felt a great relief in these miles of heath and the sense of holiday that they gave him. But all the joy round him and in his heart found their point for him in the person that went with him; this presence was their centre, as a diamond in a gold ring, or as a throned figure in a Court circle. All else existed for the sake of this person;—the heather blossomed and the gorse incensed the air, and the sea sparkled, and the sky was blue, and the air kindled, and his own heart warmed and throbbed, for that only. When he tried to see who it was, there was nothing to see; the presence existed there as a centre in a sphere, immeasurable and indiscernible; sometimes he thought it was Mary, sometimes he thought it Henry Buxton, sometimes Isabel—once even he assured himself it was Mistress Margaret, and once James Maxwell—and with the very act of identification came indecision again. This uncertainty waxed into a torment, and yet a sweet torment, as of a lover who watches his mistress' shuttered house; and this torment swelled yet higher and deeper until it was so great that it had absorbed the whole radiant fragrant circle of the hills where he walked; and then came the blinding knowledge that the Presence was all these persons so dear to him, and far more; that every tenderness and grace that he had loved in them—Mary's gallantry and Isabel's serene silence and his friend's fellowship, and the rest—floated in the translucent depths of it, stained and irradiated by it, as motes in a sunbeam.

And then he woke, and it was through tears of pure joy that he saw the rafters overhead, and the great barred door, and the discoloured wall above his bed.

When his gaoler brought him dinner that day it was half an hour earlier than usual; and when Anthony asked him the reason he said that he did not know, but that the orders had run so; but that Mr. Norris might take heart; it was not for the torture, for Mr. Topcliffe, who superintended it, had told the keeper of the rack-house that nothing would be wanted that day.

He had hardly finished dinner when the gaoler came up again and said that the Lieutenant was waiting for him below, and that he must bring his hat and cloak.

Since his arrest he had worn his priest's habit every day, so he now threw the cloak over his arm and took his hat, and followed the gaoler down.

In passing through the court he went by a group of men that were talking together, and he noticed very especially a tall old man with a grey head, in a Court suit with a sword, and very lean about the throat, who looked at him hard as he passed. As he reached the archway where the Lieutenant was waiting, he turned again and saw the sunken eyes of the old man still looking after him; when he turned to the gaoler he saw the same odd look in his face that he had noticed before.

"Why do you look like that?" he asked. "Who is that old man?"

"That is Mr. Topcliffe," said the keeper.

The Lieutenant of the Tower, Sir Richard Barkley, saluted him kindly at the gate, and begged him to follow him; the keeper still came after and another stepped out and joined them, and the group of four together passed out through the Lion's Tower and across the moat to a little doorway where a closed carriage was waiting. The Lieutenant and Anthony stepped inside; the two keepers mounted outside; and the carriage set off.

Then the Lieutenant turned to the priest.

"Do you know where you are going, Mr. Norris?"

"No, sir."

"You are going to Whitehall to see the Queen's Grace."

CHAPTER XIV
AN OPEN DOOR

When the carriage reached the palace they were told that the Queen was not yet come from Greenwich; and they were shown into a little anteroom next the gallery where the interview was to take place. The Queen, the Lieutenant told Anthony, was to come up that afternoon passing through London, and that she had desired to see him on her way through to Nonsuch; he could not tell him why he was sent for, though he conjectured it was because of Mistress Corbet's death, and that her Grace wished to know the details.

"However," said the Lieutenant, "you now have your opportunity to speak for yourself, and I think you a very fortunate man, Mr. Norris. Few have had such a privilege, though I remember that Mr. Campion had it too, though he made poor use of it."

Anthony said nothing. His mind was throbbing with memories and associations. The air of state and luxury in the corridors through which he had just come, the discreet guarded doors, the servants in the royal liveries standing here and there, the sense of expectancy that mingled with the solemn hush of the palace—all served to bring up the figure of Mary Corbet, whom he had seen so often in these circumstances; and the thought of her made the peril in which he stood and the hope of escape from it seem very secondary matters. He walked to the window presently and looked out upon the little court below, one of the innumerable yards of that vast palace, and stood staring down on the hound that was chained there near one of the entrances, and that yawned and blinked in the autumn sunshine.

Even as he looked the dog paused in the middle of his stretch and stood expectant with his ears cocked, a servant dashed bareheaded down a couple of steps and out through the low archway; and simultaneously Anthony heard once more the sweet shrill trumpets that told of the Queen's approach; then there came the roll of drums and the thunder of horses' feet and the noise of wheels; the trumpets sang out again nearer, and the rumbling waxed louder as the Queen's cavalcade, out of sight, passed the entrance of the archway down upon which Anthony looked; and then stilled, and the palace itself began to hum and stir; a door or two banged in the distance, feet ran past the door of the ante-room, and the strain of the trumpets sounded once in the house itself. Then all grew quiet once more, and Anthony turned from the window and sat down again by the Lieutenant.

There was silence for a few minutes. The Lieutenant stroked his beard gently and said a word or two under his breath now and again to Anthony; once or twice there came the swift rustle of a dress outside as a lady hurried past; then the sound of a door opening and shutting; then more silence; then the sound of low talking, and at last the sound of footsteps going slowly up and down the gallery which adjoined the ante-room.

Still the minutes passed, but no summons came. Anthony rose and went to the window again, for, in spite of himself, this waiting told upon him. The dog had gone back to his kennel and was lying with his nose just outside the opening. Anthony wondered vacantly to himself what door it was that he was guarding, and who lived in the rooms that looked out beside it. Then suddenly the door from the gallery opened and a page appeared.

"The Queen's Grace will see Mr. Norris alone."

Anthony went towards him, and the page opened the door wide for him to go through, and then closed it noiselessly behind him, and Anthony was in the presence.

It was with a sudden bewilderment that he recognised he was in the same gallery as that in which he had talked and sat with Mary Corbet. There were the long tapestries hanging opposite him, with the tall three windows dividing them, and the suits of steel armour that he remembered. He even recalled the pattern of the carpet across which Mary Corbet had come forward to meet him, and that still lay before the tall window at the end that looked on to the Tilt-yard. The sun was passing round to the west now, and shone again across the golden haze of the yard through this great window, with the fragments of stained glass at the top. The memory leapt into life even as he stepped out and stood for a moment, dazed in the sunshine, at the door that opened from the ante-room.

But the figure that turned from the window and faced him was not like Mary's. It was the figure of an old woman, who looked tall with her towering head-dress and nodding plume; she was dressed in a great dark red mantle thrown back on her shoulders, and beneath it was a pale yellow dress sown all over with queer devices; on the puffed sleeve of the arm that held the stick was embroidered a great curling snake that shone with gold thread and jewels in the sunlight, and powdered over the skirt were representations of human eyes and other devices, embroidered with dark thread that showed up plainly on the pale ground. So much he saw down one side of the figure on which the light shone; the rest was to his dazzled eyes in dark shadow. He went down on his knees at once before this tremendous figure, seeing the buckled feet that twinkled below the skirt cut short in front, and remained there.

There was complete silence for a moment, while he felt the Queen looking at him, and then the voice he remembered, only older and harsher, now said:

"What is all this, Mr. Norris?"

Anthony looked for a moment and saw the Queen's eyes fixed on him; but he said nothing, and looked down again.

"Stand up," said the Queen, not unkindly, "and walk with me."

Anthony stood up at once, and heard the stiff rustle of her dress and the tap of her heels and stick on the polished boards as she came towards him. Then he turned with her down the long gallery.

Until this moment, ever since he had heard that he was to see the Queen, he had felt nervous and miserable; but now this had left him, and he felt at his ease. To be received in this way, in privacy, and to accompany her up and down the gallery as she took her afternoon exercise was less embarrassing than the formal interview he had expected. The two walked the whole length of the gallery without a word, and it was not until they turned and faced the end that looked on to the Tilt-yard that the Queen spoke; and her voice was almost tender.

"I understand that you were with Minnie Corbet when she died," she said.

"She died for me, your Grace," said Anthony.

The Queen looked at him sharply.

"Tell me the tale," she said.

And Anthony told her the whole story of the escape and the ride; speaking too for his friend, Mr. Buxton, and of Mary's affection for him.

"Your Grace," he ended, "it sounds a poor tale of a man that a woman should die for him so; but I can say with truth that with God's grace I would have died a hundred deaths to save her."

The Queen was silent for a good while when the story was over, and Anthony thought that perhaps she could not speak; but he dared not look at her.

Then she spoke very harshly:

"And you, Mr. Norris, why did you not escape?"

"Your Grace would not have done so."

"When I saw that she was dying, I would."

"Not if you had been a priest, your Grace."

"What is that?" asked the Queen, suddenly facing him.

"I am a priest, madam, and she was a Catholic, and my duty was beside her."

"Eh?"

"I shrived her, your Grace, before she died."

"Why! they did not tell me that."

Anthony was silent.

They walked on a few steps, and the Queen stood silent too, looking down upon the Tilt-yard. Then she turned abruptly, and Anthony turned with her, and they began to go up and down again.

"It was gallant of you both," she said shortly. "I love that my people should be of that sort." Then she paused. "Tell me," she went on, "did Mary love me?"

Anthony was silent for a moment.

"The truth, Mr. Norris," she said.

"Mistress Corbet was loyalty itself," he answered.

"Nay, nay, nay, not loyalty but love I asked you of. How did she speak of me?"

"Well, your Grace, Mistress Corbet had a shrewd wit, and she used it freely on friend and foe, but her very sharpness on your Grace, sometimes, showed her love; for she hated to think you otherwise than what she deemed the best."

The Queen stopped full in her walk.

"That is very pleasantly put," she said; "I told Minnie you were a courtier."

Again the two walked on.

"Then she used her tongue on me?"

"Your Grace, I have never met one on whom she did not: but her heart was true."

"I know that, I know that, Mr. Norris. Tell me something she said."

Anthony racked his brains for something not too severe.

"Mistress Corbet once said that the Queen's most disobedient subject was herself."

"Eh?" said Elizabeth, stopping in her walk.

"'Because,' said Mistress Corbet, 'she can never command herself,'" finished Anthony.

The Queen looked at Anthony, puzzled a moment; and then chuckled loudly in her throat.

"The impertinent minx!" she said, "that was when I had clouted her, no doubt."

Again they walked up and down in silence a little while. Anthony began to wonder whether this was all for which the Queen had sent for him. He was astonished at his own self-possession; all the trembling awe with which he had faced the Queen at Greenwich was gone; he had forgotten for the moment even his own peril; and he felt instead even something of pity for this passionate old woman, who had aged so quickly, whose favourites one by one were dropping off, or at the best giving her only an exaggerated and ridiculous devotion, at the absurdity of which all the world laughed. Here was this old creature at his side, surrounded by flatterers and adventurers, advancing through the world in splendid and jewelled raiment, with trumpets blowing before her, and poets singing her praises, and crowds applauding in the streets, and sneering in their own houses at the withered old virgin-Queen who still thought herself a Diana—and all the while this triumphal progress was at the expense of God's Church, her car rolled over the bodies of His servants, and her shrunken, gemmed fingers were red in their blood;—so she advanced, thought Anthony, day by day towards the black truth and the eternal loneliness of the darkness that lies outside the realm where Christ only is King.

Elizabeth broke in suddenly on his thoughts.

"Now," she said, "and what of you, Mr. Norris?"

"I am your Grace's servant," he said.

"I am not so sure of that," said Elizabeth. "If you are my servant, why are you a priest, contrary to my laws?"

"Because I am Christ's servant too, your Grace."

"But Christ's apostle said, 'Obey them that have the rule over you.'"

"In indifferent matters, madam."

The Queen frowned and made a little angry sound.

"I cannot understand you Papists," said the Queen. "What a-God's name do you want? You have liberty of thought and faith; I desire to inquire into no man's private opinions. You may worship Ashtaroth if it please you, in your own hearts; and God looks to the heart, and not to the outer man. There is a Church with bishops like your own, and ministers; there are the old churches to worship in—nay, you may find the old ornaments still in use. We have sacraments as you have; you may seek shrift if you will; nay, in some manner we have the mass—though we do not call it so—but we follow Christ's ordinance in the matter, and you can do no more. We have the Word of God as you have, and we use the same creeds. What more can the rankest Papist ask? Tell me that, Mr. Norris; for I am a-weary of your folk."

The Queen turned and faced him again a moment, and her eyes were peevish and resentful.

Presently she went on again.

"Mr. Campion told me it was the oath that troubled him. He could not take it, he said. I told the fool that I was not Head of the Church as Christ was, but only the supreme governor, as the Act declares, in all spiritual and ecclesiastical things:—I forget how it runs,—but I showed it him, and asked him whether it were not true; and I asked him too how it was that Margaret Roper could take the oath, and so many thousands of persons as full Christian as himself—and he could not answer me."

The Queen was silent again. Then once more she went on indignantly:

"It is yourselves that have brought all this trouble on your heads. See what the Papists have done against me; they have excommunicated me, deposed me—though in spite of it I still sit on the throne; they have sent an Armada against me; they have plotted against me, I know not how many times; and then, when I defend myself and hang a few of the wolves, lo! they are Christ's flock at once for whom he shed His precious blood, and His persecuted lambs, and I am Jezebel straightway and Athaliah and Beelzebub's wife—and I know not what."

The Queen stopped, out of breath, and looked fiercely at Anthony, who said nothing.

"Tell me how you answer that, Mr. Norris?" said the Queen.

"I dare not deal with such great matters," said Anthony, "for your Grace knows well that I am but a poor priest that knows nought of state-craft; but I would like to ask your Highness two questions only. The first is: whether your Grace had aught to complain of in the conduct of your

Catholic subjects when the Armada was here; and the second, whether there hath been one actual attempt upon your Grace's life by private persons?"

"That is not to the purpose," said the Queen peevishly.

"It was Catholics who fought against me in the Armada, and it was Catholics who plotted against me at Court."

"Then there is a difference in Catholics, your Grace," said Anthony.

"Ah! I see what you would be at."

"Yes, your Highness; I would rather say, Although they be Catholics they do these things."

There was silence again, which Anthony did not dare to break; and the two walked up the whole length of the gallery without speaking.

"Well, well," said Elizabeth at last, "but this was not why I sent for you. We will speak of yourself now, Mr. Norris. I hope you are not an obstinate fellow. Eh?"

Anthony said nothing, and the Queen went on.

"Now, as I have told you, I judge no man's private opinions. You may believe what you will. Remember that. You may believe what you will; nay, you may practise your religion so long as it is private and unknown to me."

Anthony began to wonder what was coming; but he still said nothing as the Queen paused. She stood a moment looking down into the empty Tilt-yard again, and then turned and sat suddenly in a chair that stood beside the window, and put up a jewelled hand to shield her face, with her elbow on the arm, while Anthony stood before her.

"I remember you, Mr. Norris, very well at Greenwich; you spoke up sharply enough, and you looked me in the eyes now and then as I like a man to do; and then Minnie loved you, too. I wish to show you kindness for her sake."

Anthony's heart began to fail him, for he guessed now what was coming and the bitter struggle that lay before him.

"Now, I know well that the Commissioners have had you before them; they are tiresome busybodies. Walsingham started all that and set them a-spying and a-defending of my person and the rest of it; but they are loyal folk, and I suppose they asked you where you had been and with whom you had stayed, and so on?"

"They did, your Grace."

"And you would not tell them, I suppose?"

"I could not, madam; it would have been against justice and charity to do so."

"Well, well, there is no need now, for I mean to take you out of their hands."

A great leap of hope made itself felt in Anthony's heart; he did not know how heavy the apprehension lay on him till this light shone through.

"They will be wrath with me, I know, and will tell me that they cannot defend me if I will not help them; but, when all is said, I am Queen. Now I do not ask you to be a minister of my Church, for that, I think, you would never be; but I think you would like to be near me—is it not so? And I wish you to have some post about the Court; I must see what it is to be."

Anthony's heart began to sink again as he watched the Queen's face as she sat tapping a foot softly and looking on the floor as she talked. Those lines of self-will about the eyes and mouth surely meant something.

Then she looked up, still with her cheek on her right hand.

"You do not thank me, Mr. Norris."

Anthony made a great effort; but he heard his own voice quiver a little.

"I thank your Grace for your kindly intentions toward me, with all my heart."

The Queen seemed satisfied, and looked down again.

"As to the oath, I will not ask you to take it formally, if you will give me an assurance of your loyalty."

"That, your Grace, I give most gladly."

His heart was beating again in great irregular thumps in his throat; he had the sensation of swaying to and fro on the edge of a precipice, now towards safety and now towards death; it was the cruellest pain he had suffered yet. But how was it possible to have some post at Court without relinquishing the exercise of his priesthood? He must think it out; what did the Queen mean?

"And, of course, you will not be able to say mass again; but I shall not hinder your hearing it at the Ambassador's whenever you please."

Ah! it had come; his heart gave a leap and seemed to cease.

"Your Grace must forgive me, but I cannot consent."

There was a dead silence; when Anthony looked up, she was staring at him with the frankest astonishment.

"Did you think, Mr. Norris, you could be at Court and say mass too whenever you wished?" Her voice rang harsh and shrill; her anger was rising.

"I was not sure what your Grace intended for me."

"The fellow is mad," she said, still staring at him. "Oh! take care, take care!"

"Your Grace knows I intend no insolence."

"You mean to say, Mr. Norris, that you will not take a pardon and a post at Court on those terms?"

Anthony bowed; he could not trust himself to speak, so bitter was the reaction.

"But, see man, you fool; if you die as a traitor you will never say mass again either."

"But that will not be with my consent, your Grace."

"And you refuse the pardon?"

"On those terms, your Grace, I must."

"Well— —" and she was silent a moment, "you are a fool, sir."

Anthony bowed again.

"But I like courage.—Well, then, you will not be my servant?"

"I have ever been that, your Grace; and ever will be."

"Well, well,—but not at Court?"

"Ah! your Grace knows I cannot," cried Anthony, and his voice rang sorrowfully.

Again there was silence.

"You must have your way, sir, for poor Minnie's sake; but it passes my understanding what you mean by it. And let me tell you that not many have their way with me, rather than mine."

Again hope leapt up in his heart. The Queen then was not so ungracious.

He looked up and smiled—and down again.

"Why, the man's lips are all a-quiver. What ails him?"

"It is your Grace's kindness."

"I must say I marvel at it myself," observed Elizabeth. "You near angered me just now; take care you do not so quite."

"I would not willingly, as your Grace knows."

"Then we will end this matter. You give me your assurance of loyalty to my person."

"With all my heart, madam," said Anthony eagerly.

"Then you must get to France within the week. The other too—Buxton—he loses his estate, but has his life. I am doing much for Minnie's sake."

"How can I thank your Grace?"

"And I will cause Sir Richard to give it out that you have taken the oath. Call him in."

There was a quick gasp from the priest; and then he cried with agony in his voice:

"I cannot, your Grace, I cannot."

"Cannot call Sir Richard! Why, you are mad, sir!"

"Cannot consent; I have taken no oath."

"I know you have not. I do not ask it."

Elizabeth's voice came short and harsh; her patience was vanishing, and Anthony knew it and looked at her. She had dropped her hand, and it was clenching and unclenching on her knee. Her stick slipped on the polished boards and fell; but she paid it no attention. She was looking straight at the priest; her high eyebrows were coming down; her mouth was beginning to mumble a little; he could see in the clear sunlight that fell on her sideways through the tall window a thousand little wrinkles, and all seemed alive; the lines at the corners of her eyes and mouth deepened as he watched.

"What a-Christ's name do you want, sir?"

It was like the first mutter of a storm on the horizon; but Anthony knew it must break. He did not answer.

"Tell me, sir; what is it now?"

Anthony drew a long breath and braced his will, but even as he spoke he knew he was pronouncing his own sentence.

"I cannot consent to leave the country and let it be given out that I had taken the oath, your Grace. It would be an apostasy from my faith."

Elizabeth sprang to her feet without her stick, took one step forward, and gave Anthony a fierce blow on the cheek with her ringed hand. He recoiled a step at the shock of it, and stood waiting with his eyes on the ground. Then the Queen's anger poured out in words. Her eyes burned with passion out of an ivory-coloured face, and her voice rang high and harsh, and her hands continually clenched and unclenched as she screamed at him.

"God's Body! you are the ungratefullest hound that ever drew breath. I send for you to my presence, and talk and walk with you like a friend. I offer you a pardon and you fling it in my face. I offer you a post at Court and you mock it; you flaunt you in your treasonable livery in my very face, and laugh at my clemency. You think I am no Queen, but a weak woman whom you can turn and rule at your will. God's Son! I will show you which is sovereign. Call Sir Richard in, sir; I will have him in this instant. Sir Richard, Sir Richard!" she screamed, stamping with fury.

The door into the ante-room behind opened, and Sir Richard Barkley appeared, with a face full of apprehension. He knelt at once.

"Stand up, Sir Richard," she cried, "and look at this man. You know him, do you not? and I know him now, the insolent dog! But his own mother shall not in a week. Look at him shaking there, the knave; he will shake more before I have done with him. Take him back with you, Sir Richard, and let them have their will of him. His damned pride and insolence shall be broken. S' Body, I have never been so treated! Take him out, Sir Richard, take him out, I tell you!"

CHAPTER XV
THE ROLLING OF THE STONE

It was a week later, and a little before dawn, that Isabel was kneeling by Anthony's bed in his room in the Tower. The Lieutenant had sent for her to his lodging the evening before, and she had spent the whole night with her brother. He had been racked four times in one week, and was dying.

The city and the prison were very quiet now; the carts had not yet begun to roll over the cobble-stones and the last night-wanderers had gone home. He lay, on the mattress that she had sent in to him, in the corner of his cell under the window, on his back and very still, covered from chin to feet with her own fur-lined cloak that she had thrown over him; his head was on a low pillow, for he could not bear to lie high; his feet made a little mound under the coverlet, and his arms lay straight at his side; but all that could be seen of him was his face, pinched and white now with hollows in his cheeks and dark patches and lines beneath his closed eyes, and his soft pointed brown beard that just rested on the fur edging of Isabel's cloak; his lips were drawn tight, but slightly parted, showing the rim of his white teeth, as if he snarled with pain.

The only furniture in the room was a single table and chair; the table was drawn up not far from the bed, and a book or two, with a flask of cordial and some fragments of food on a plate lay upon it; his cloak and doublet and ruff lay across the chair and his shoes below it, and a little linen lay in a pile in another corner; but the clothes in which he had been tortured the evening before, his shirt and hose, could not be taken off him and he lay in them still. They had been so soaked with sweat, that Isabel had found him shivering, and laid her cloak over him, and now he lay quiet and warm.

Earlier in the night she had been reading to him, and a taper still burned in a candlestick on the table; but for the last two hours he had lain either in a sleep or a swoon, and she had laid the book down and was watching him.

He was so motionless that he would have seemed dead except for the steady rise and fall of a fold in the mantle, and for a sudden muscular twitch every few minutes. Isabel herself was scarcely less motionless; her face was clear and pale as it always was, but perfectly serene, and even her lips did not quiver. She was kneeling and leaning back now, and her hands were clasped in her lap. There was a proud content in her face; her dear brother had not uttered one name on the rack except those of the Saviour and of the Blessed Mother. So the Lieutenant had told her.

Suddenly his eyes opened and there was nothing but peace in them; and his lips moved. Isabel leaned forward on her hands and bent her ear to his mouth till his breath was warm on it, and she could hear the whisper....

Then she opened the book that lay face down on the table and began to read on, from the point at which she had laid it down two hours before.

"'*Erat autem hora tertia: et crucifixerunt eum.* And it was the third hour and they crucified him ... And with him they crucify two thieves, the one on his right hand, and the other on his left. And the scripture was fulfilled which saith, And he was numbered with the transgressors.'"

Her voice was slow and steady as she read the unfamiliar Latin, still kneeling, with the book a little raised to catch the candlelight, and her grave tranquil eyes bent upon it. Only once did her voice falter, and then she commanded it again immediately; and that, as she read "*Erant autem et mulieres de longe aspicientes.*" "There were also women looking on afar off."

And so the tale crept on, minute by minute, and the priest lay with closed eyes to hear it; until the mocking was complete, and the darkness of the sixth hour had come and gone, and the Saviour had cried aloud on His Father, and given up the ghost; and the centurion that stood by had borne witness. And the great Criminal slept in the garden, in the sepulchre "wherein was never man yet laid."

There was a listening silence as the voice ceased without another falter. Isabel laid the book down and looked at him again; and his eyes opened languidly.

He had not yet said more than single words, and even now his voice was so faint that she had to put her ear close to his mouth. It seemed to her that his soul had gone into some inner secret chamber of profound peace, so deep that it was a long and difficult task to send a thought to the surface through his lips.

She could just hear him, and she answered clearly and slowly as to a dazed child, pausing between every word.

"I cannot get a priest; it is not allowed."

Still his eyes bent on her; what was it he said? what was it?...

Then she heard, and began to repeat short acts of contrition clearly and distinctly, pausing between the phrases, in English, and his eyes closed as she began:

"O my Jesus—I am heartily sorry—that I have—crucified thee—by my sins—Wash my soul—in Thy Precious Blood. O my God—I am sorry—that I have—displeased Thee—because thou art All-good. I hate all the sins—that I have done—against Thy Divine Majesty."

And so phrase after phrase she went on, giving him time to hear and to make an inner assent of the will; and repeating also other short vocal prayers that she knew by heart. And so the delicate skein of prayer rose from the altar where this morning sacrifice lay before God, waiting the consummation of His acceptance.

Presently she ended, and he lay again with closed eyes and mute face. Then again they opened, and she bent down to listen....

"It will all be well with me," she answered, raising her head again. "Mistress Margaret has written from Brussels. I shall go there for a while.... Yes, Mr. Buxton will take me; next week: he goes to Normandy, to his estate."

Again his lips moved and she listened....

A faint flush came over her face. She shook her head.

"I do not know; I think not. I hope to enter Religion.... No, I have not yet determined.... The Dower House?... Yes, I will sell it.... Yes, to Hubert, if he wishes it."

Every word he whispered was such an effort that she had to pause again and again before he could make her understand; and often she judged more by the movement of his lips than by any sound that came from him. Now and then too she lifted her handkerchief, soaked in a strong violet scent, and passed it over his forehead and lips. She motioned with the flask of cordial once or twice, but his eyes closed for a negative.

As she knelt and watched him, her thoughts circled continually in little flights; to the walled garden of the Dower House in sunshine, and Anthony running across it in his brown suit, with the wallflowers behind him against the old red bricks and ivy, and the tall chestnut rising behind; to the windswept hills, with the thistles and the golden-rod, and the hazel thickets, and Anthony on his pony, sunburnt and voluble, hawk on wrist, with a light in his eyes; to the warm panelled hall in winter, with the tapers on the round table, and Anthony flat on his face, with his feet in the air before the hearth, that glowed and roared up the wide chimney behind, and his chin on his hands, and a book open before him; or, farther back even still, to Anthony's little room at the top of the house, his clothes on a chair, and the boy himself sitting up in bed with his arms round his knees as she came in to wish him good-night and talk to him a minute or two. And every time the circling thought came home and settled again on the sight of that still straight figure lying on the mattress, against the discoloured bricks, with the light of the taper glimmering on his thin face and brown hair and beard; and every time her heart consented that this was the best of all.

A bird chirped suddenly from some hole in the Tower, once, and then three or four times; she glanced up at the window and the light of dawn was beginning. Then, as the minutes went by, the city began to stir itself from sleep. There came a hollow whine from the Lion-gate fifty yards away; up from the river came the shout of a waterman; two or three times a late cock crew; and still the light crept on and broadened. But Anthony still lay with his eyes closed.

At last over the cobbles outside a cart rattled, turned a corner and was silent. Anthony had opened his eyes now and was looking at her again; and again she bent down to listen; ... and then opened and read again.

"'*Et cum transisset sabbatum Maria Magdalene et Maria Jacobi et Salome emerunt aromata, ut venientes ungerent Jesum.*'

"'And when the Sabbath was past, Mary Magdalene and Mary the mother of James and Salome, had bought sweet spices that they might come and anoint him.'"

A slight sound made her look up. Anthony's eyes were kindling and his lips moved; she bent again and listened.... What was it he said?...

Yes, it was so, and she smiled and nodded at him: she was reading the Gospel for Easter Day, the Gospel of the first mass that they had heard together on that spring morning at Great Keynes, when their Lord had led them so far round by separate paths to meet one another at His altar. And now they were met again here. She read on:

"'*Et valde mane una sabbatorum, veniunt ad monumentum, orto jam sole.*'

"'Very early they came unto the sepulchre at the rising of the sun; and they said among themselves, Who shall roll us away the stone from the door of the sepulchre? And when they looked, they saw that the stone was rolled away, for it was very great.'...

"'... *magnus valde*,'" read Isabel; and looked up again;—and then closed the book. There was no need to read more.

She walked across the court half an hour later, just as the sun came up; and passed out through the Lieutenant's lodging, and out by the narrow bridge on to the Tower wharf.

To the left and behind her, as she looked eastwards down the river, lay the heavy masses of the prison she had left, and the high walls and turrets were gilded with glory. The broad river itself was one rolling glory too; the tide was coming in swift and strong and a barge or two moved upwards, only half seen in the bewildering path of the sun. The air was cool and keen, and a breeze from the water stirred Isabel's hair as she stood looking, with the light on her face. It was a cloudless October morning overhead. Even as she stood a flock of pigeons streamed across from the south side, swift-flying and bathed in light; and her eyes followed them a moment or two.

As she stood there silent, a step came up the wharf from the direction of St. Katharine's street, and a man came walking quickly towards her. He did not see who she was until he was close, and then he started and took off his hat; it was Lackington on his way to some business at the Tower; but she did not seem to see him. She turned almost immediately and began to walk westwards, and the glory in her eyes was supreme. And as she went the day deepened above her.